TENTERHOOKS

by the same author

The Twelfth Hour (1907)

Love's Shadow (1908)

The Limit (1911)

Tenterhooks (1912)

Bird of Paradise (1914)

Love at Second Sight (1916)

Letters to the Sphinx from Oscar Wilde
with Reminiscences of the Author (1930)

TENTERHOOKS

by

ADA LEVERSON

ADELAIDE
MICHAEL WALMER
2019

Tenterhooks first published 1912
This edition published 2019

by

Michael Walmer
9/2 Dahlmyra Avenue
Hamley Bridge
South Australia 5401

ISBN 978-0-6485905-4-5 paperback

ERRATA
This edition has been prepared utilizing a previous edition; thus errors have been reproduced. On page 23, line 8, for *Burce* please read *Bruce*; on page 33, line 28, for *Mi s* please read *Miss*; on page 55, line 25, for *moking* please read *smoking*; on page 81, line 17, for *Bohem ans* please read *Bohemians*; on page 101, line 4, for *outl ne* please read *outline*; and on page 103, line 3, for *l ghtness* please read *lightness*.

TO
ROBERT ROSS

CONTENTS

CHAPTER	PAGE
I. A VERBAL INVITATION	9
II. OPERA GLASSES	21
III. THE GOLDEN QUORIBUS	31
IV. THE MITCHELLS	39
V. THE SURPRISE	50
VI. THE VISIT	58
VII. COUP DE FOUDRE	67
VIII. ARCHIE'S ESSAY	77
IX. AYLMER	81
X. SHOPPING CHEZ SOI	95
XI. P.P.C.	106
XII. "THE MOONSHINE GIRL"	111
XIII. THE SUPPER-PARTY	121
XIV. THE LETTER	131
XV. MAVIS ARGLES	139
XVI. MORE OF THE MITCHELLS	151

CHAPTER	PAGE
XVII. THE AGONIES OF AYLMER	159
XVIII. A CONTRETEMPS	168
XIX. AN EXTRAORDINARY AFTERNOON	175
XX. JOURNEYS END	185
XXI. THE GREAT EXCEPTION	189
XXII. ANOTHER SIDE OF BRUCE	202
XXIII. AT LADY EVERARD'S	216
XXIV. MISS BENNETT	231
XXV. AT WESTGATE	238
XXVI. GOGGLES	244
XXVII. THE ELOPEMENT	251
XXVIII. BRUCE RETURNS	263
XXIX. INTELLECTUAL SYMPATHY	275

CHAPTER I

A VERBAL INVITATION

BECAUSE Edith had not been feeling very well, that seemed no reason why she should be the centre of interest; and Bruce, with that jealousy of the privileges of the invalid and in that curious spirit of rivalry which his wife had so often observed, had started, with enterprise, an indisposition of his own, as if to divert public attention. While he was at Carlsbad he heard the news. Then he received a letter from Edith, speaking with deference and solicitude of Bruce's rheumatism, entreating him to do the cure thoroughly, and suggesting that they should call the little girl Matilda, after a rich and sainted—though still living—aunt of Edith's. It might be an advantage to the child's future (in every sense) to have a godmother so wealthy and so religious. It appeared from the detailed description that the new daughter had, as a matter of course (and at two days old), long golden hair, far below her waist, sweeping lashes and pencilled brows, a rosebud mouth, an intellectual forehead, chiselled features and a tall, elegant figure. She was a magnificent, regal-looking creature and was a superb beauty of the classic type, and yet with it she was dainty and winsome. She had great talent for music. This, it appeared, was shown by the breadth between the eyes and the timbre of her voice.

Overwhelmed with joy at the advent of such a paragon, and horrified at Edith's choice of a name, Bruce had replied at once by wire, impulsively:

"*Certainly not Matilda I would rather she were called Aspasia.*"

Edith read this expression of feeling on a colourless telegraph form, and as she was, at Knightsbridge, unable to hear the ironical tone of the message she took it literally.

She criticised the name, but was easily persuaded by her mother-in-law to make no objection. The elder Mrs. Ottley pointed out that it might have been very much worse.

"But it's not a pretty name," objected Edith. "If it wasn't to be Matilda, I should rather have called her something out of Maeterlinck—Ygraine, or Ysolyn—something like that."

"Yes, dear, Mygraine's a nice name, too," said Mrs. Ottley, in her humouring way, "and so is Vaselyn. But what does it really matter? I shouldn't hold out on a point like this. One gets used to a name. Let the poor child be called Asparagus if he wishes it, and let him feel he has got his own way."

So the young girl was named Aspasia Matilda Ottley. It was characteristic of Edith that she kept to her own point, though not aggressively. When Bruce returned after his after-cure, it was too late to do anything but pretend he had meant it seriously.

Archie called his sister Dilly.

Archie had been rather hurt at the—as it seemed to him—unnecessary excitement about Dilly. Not that he was jealous in any way. It was rather that he was afraid it would spoil her to be made so much of at her age; make her, perhaps, egotistical and vain. But it was not Archie's way to show these fears openly. He did not weep loudly or throw things about as many boys might have done. His methods were more roundabout, more subtle. He gave hints and suggestions of his views that should have been understood by the intelligent. He said one morning with some indirectness:

"I had such a lovely dream last night, mother."

"Did you, pet? How sweet of you. What was it?"

"Oh, nothing much. It was all right. Very nice. It was a lovely dream. I dreamt I was in heaven."

"Really! How delightful. Who was there?"

This is always a woman's first question.

"Oh, you were there, of course. And father. Nurse, too. It was a lovely dream. Such a nice place".

"Was Dilly there?"

"Dilly? Er—no—no—she wasn't. She was in the night nursery, with Satan."

Sometimes Edith thought that her daughter's names were decidedly a failure—Aspasia by mistake, Matilda through obstinacy, and Dilly by accident. However the child herself was a success. She was four years old when the incident occurred about the Mitchells. The whole of this story turns eventually on the Mitchells.

The Ottleys lived in a concise white flat at Knightsbridge. Bruce's father had some time ago left him a good income on certain conditions; one was that he was not to leave the Foreign Office before he was fifty.

One afternoon Edith was talking to the telephone in a voice of agonised entreaty that would have melted the hardest of hearts, but

A VERBAL INVITATION

did not seem to have much effect on the Exchange, which, evidently, was not responsive to pathos that day.

"Oh! Exchange, *why* are you ringing off? *Please* try again. ... Do I want any number? Yes, I do want any number, of course, or why should I ring up? ... I want 6375 Gerrard."

Here Archie interposed.

"Mother, can I have your long buttonhook?"

"No, Archie, you can't just now, dear. ... Go away, Archie. ... Yes, I said 6375 Gerrard. Only 6375 Gerrard! ... Are you there? Oh, *don't* keep on asking me if I've got them! ... No, they *haven't* answered. ... Are you 6375? ... Oh—wrong number—sorry. ... 6375 Gerrard? Only six—are you there? ... Not 6375 Gerrard? ... Are you anyone else? ... Oh, is it you, Vincy? ... I want to tell you——"

"Mother, can I have your long buttonhook?"

Here Bruce came in. Edith rang off. Archie disappeared.

"It's really rather wonderful, Edith, what that Sandow exerciser has done for me! You laughed at me at first, but I've improved marvellously."

Bruce was walking about doing very mild gymnastics, and occasionally hitting himself on the left arm with the right fist. "Look at my muscle—look at it—and all in such a short time!"

"Wonderful!" said Edith.

"The reason I know what an extraordinary effect these few days have had on me is something I have just done which I couldn't have done before. Of course I'm naturally a very powerful man, and only need a little——"

"What have you done?"

"Why—you know that great ridiculous old wooden chest that your awful Aunt Matilda sent you for you birthday—absurd present I call it—mere lumber."

"Yes?"

"When it came I could barely push it from one side of the room to the other. Now I've lifted it from your room to the box-room. Quite easily. Pretty good, isn't it?"

"Yes, of course it's very good for you to do all these exercises; no doubt it's capital. . . . Er—you know I've had all the things taken out of the chest since you tried it before, don't you?"

'Things—what things? I didn't know there was anything in it."

"Only a silver tea-service, and a couple of salvers," said Edith, in a low voice. . . .

. . . He calmed down fairly soon and said:

"Edith, I have some news for you. You know the Mitchells?"

"Do I know the *Mitchells*? Mitchell, your hero in your office, that you're always being offended with—at *least* I know the Mitchells by *name*. I ought to."

"Well, what do you think they've done? They've asked us to dinner."

"Have they? Fancy!"

"Yes, and what I thought was so particularly jolly of him was that it was a verbal invitation. Mitchell said to me, just like this, 'Ottley, old chap, are you doing anything on Sunday evening?'"

Here Archie came to the door and said, "Mother, can I have your long buttonhook?"

Edith shook her head and frowned.

"'Ottley, old chap,'" continued Bruce, "'are you and your wife doing anything on Sunday? If not, I do wish you would waive ceremony and come and dine with us. Would Mrs. Ottley excuse a verbal invitation, do you think?' I said, 'Well, Mitchell, as a matter of fact I don't believe we have got anything on. Yes, old boy, we shall be delighted.' I accepted, you see. I accepted straight out. When you're treated in a friendly way, I always say why be unfriendly? And Mrs. Mitchell is a charming little woman—I'm sure you'd like her. It seems she's been dying to know you."

"Fancy! I wonder she's still alive, then, because you and Mitchell have known each other for eight years, and I've never met her yet."

"Well, you will now. Let bygones be bygones. They live in Hamilton Place."

"Oh yes. . . . Park Lane?"

"I told you he was doing very well, and his wife has private means."

"Mother," Archie began again, like a litany, "can I have your long buttonhook? I know where it is."

"No, Archie, certainly not; you can't fasten laced boots with a buttonhook. . . . Well, that will be fun, Bruce."

"I believe they're going to have games after dinner," said Bruce. "All very jolly—musical crambo—that sort of thing. . . . What shall you wear, Edith?"

"Mother, do let me have your long buttonhook. I want it. It isn't for my boots."

"*Certainly* not. What a nuisance you are! Do go away. . . . I think I shall wear my salmon-coloured dress with the sort of mayonnaise-coloured sash. . . . (No, you're not to have it, Archie.")

"But, mother, I've got it. . . . I can soon mend it, mother."

On Sunday evening Bruce's high spirits seemed to flag; he had one of his sudden reactions. He looked at everything on its dark side.

"What on earth's that thing in your hair, Edith?"

"It's a bandeau."

"I don't like it. Your hair looks very nice without it. What on *earth* did you get it for?"

"For about six-and-eleven, I think."

"Don't be trivial, Edith. We shall be late. Ah! It really does seem rather a pity, the very first time one dines with people like the Mitchells."

"We sha'n't be late, Bruce. It's eight o'clock, and eight o'clock I suppose means—well, eight. Sure you've got the number right?"

"Really. Edith! . . . My memory is unerring, dear. I never make a mistake. Haven't you ever noticed it?"

"A—oh yes—I think I have."

"Well, it's 168 Hamilton Place. Look sharp, dear."

On their way in the taxi he gave her a good many instructions and advised her to be perfectly at her ease and *absolutely natural*; there was nothing to make one otherwise, in either Mr. or Mrs. Mitchell. Also, he said, it didn't matter a bit what she wore, as long as she had put on her *best* dress. It seemed a pity she had not got a new one, but this couldn't be helped, as there was now no time. Edith agreed that she knew of no really suitable place where she could buy a new evening dress at eight-thirty on Sunday evening. And, anyhow, he said, she looked quite nice, really very smart; besides, Mrs. Mitchell was not the sort of person who would think any the less of a pretty woman for being a little dowdy and out of fashion.

When they drove up to what house agents call in their emotional way a superb, desirable, magnificent town mansion, they saw that a large dinner-party was evidently going on. A hall porter and four powdered footmen were in evidence.

"By Jove!" said Bruce, as he got out, "I'd no idea old Mitchell did himself so well as this."
... The butler had never heard of the Mitchells. The house belonged to Lord Rosenberg.

"Confound it!" said Bruce, as he flung himself into the taxi. "Well! I've made a mistake for once in my life. I admit it. Of course, it's really Hamilton Gardens. Sorry. Yet somehow I'm rather glad Mitchell doesn't live in that house."

"You are perfectly right," said Edith: "the bankruptcy of an old friend and colleague could be no satisfaction to any man."

Hamilton Gardens was a gloomy little place, like a tenement building out of Marylebone

Road. Bruce, in trying to ring the bell, unfortunately turned out all the electric light in the house, and was standing alone in despair in the dark when, fortunately, the porter, who had been out to post a letter, ran back, and turned up the light again. . . . "I shouldn't have thought they could play musical crambo here," he called out to Edith while he was waiting. "And now isn't it odd? I have a funny kind of feeling that the right address is Hamilton House."

"I suppose you're perfectly certain they don't live at a private idiot asylum?" Edith suggested doubtfully.

On inquiry it appeared the Mitchells did not live at Hamilton Gardens. An idea occurred to Edith, and she asked for a directory.

The Winthrop Mitchells lived at Hamilton Terrace, St. John's Wood.

"At last!" said Bruce. "Now we shall be too disgracefully late for the first time. But be perfectly at your ease, dear. Promise me that. Go in quite naturally."

"How else can I go in?"

"I mean as if nothing had happened."

"I think we'd better tell them what *has* happened," said Edith; "it will make them laugh. I hope they will have begun their dinner."

"Surely they will have finished it."

"Perhaps we may find them at their games!"

"Now, now, don't be bitter, Edith dear—never be bitter—life has its ups and downs.... Well! I'm rather glad, after all, that Mitchell doesn't live in that horrid little hole."

"I'm sure you are," said Edith; "it could be no possible satisfaction to you to know that a friend and colleague of yours is either distressingly hard up or painfully penurious."

They arrived at the house, but there were no lights, and no sign of life. The Mitchells lived here all right, but they were out. The parlourmaid explained. The dinner-party had been Saturday, the night before....

"Strange," said Bruce, as he got in again. "I had a curious presentiment that something was going wrong about this dinner at the Mitchells'."

"What dinner at the Mitchells'? There doesn't seem to be any."

"Do you know," Bruce continued his train of thought, "I felt certain somehow that it would be a failure. Wasn't it odd? I often think I'm a pessimist, and yet look how well I'm taking it. I'm more like a fatalist—sometimes I hardly know what I am."

"I could tell you what you are." said Edith, "but I won't, because now you must take me to the Carlton. We shall get there before it's closed."

CHAPTER II

OPERA GLASSES

WHETHER to behave with some coolness to Mitchell, and be stand-offish, as though it had been all his fault, or to be lavishly apologetic, was the question. Bruce could not make up his mind which attitude to take. In a way, it was all the Mitchells' fault. They oughtn't to have given him a verbal invitation. It was rude, Bohemian, wanting in good form; it showed an absolute and complete ignorance of the most ordinary and elementary usages of society. It was wanting in common courtesy; really, when one came to think about it, it was an insult. On the other hand, technically, Bruce was in the wrong. Having accepted he ought to have turned up on the right night. It may have served them right (as he said), but the fact of going on the wrong night being a lesson to them seemed a little obscure. Edith found it difficult to see the point.

Then he had a more brilliant idea: to go into

the office as cheerily as ever, and say to Mitchell pleasantly, "We're looking forward to next Saturday, old chap," pretending to have believed from the first that the invitation had been for the Saturday week; and that the dinner was still to come. . . .

This, Edith said, would have been excellent, provided that the parlourmaid hadn't told them that she and Bruce had arrived about a quarter to ten on Sunday evening and asked if the Mitchells had begun dinner. The chances against the servant having kept this curious incident to herself were almost too great.

After long argument and great indecision the matter was settled by a cordial letter from Mrs. Mitchell, asking them to dinner on the following Thursday, and saying she feared there had been some mistake. So that was all right.

Bruce was in good spirits again; he was pleased too, because he was going to the theatre that evening with Edith and Vincy, to see a play that he thought wouldn't be very good. He had almost beforehand settled what he thought of it, and practically what he intended to say.

But when he came in that evening he was overheard to have a strenuous and increasingly violent argument with Archie in the hall.

Edith opened the door and wanted to know what the row was about.

"Will you tell me, Edith, where your son learns such language? He keeps on worrying me to take him to the Zoological Gardens to see the —well—you'll hear what he says. The child's a perfect nuisance. Who put it into his head to want to go and see this animal? I was obliged to speak quite firmly to him about it."

Edith was not alarmed that Burce had been severe. She thought it much more likely that Archie had spoken very firmly to him. He was always strict with his father, and when he was good Bruce found fault with him. As soon as he grew really tiresome his father became abjectly apologetic.

Archie was called and came in, dragging his feet, and pouting, in tears that he was making a strenuous effort to encourage.

"You must be firm with him," continued Bruce. "Hang it! Good heavens! Am I master in my own house or am I not?"

There was no reply to this rhetorical question.

He turned to Archie and said in a gentle, conciliating voice:

"Archie, old chap, tell your mother what it is you want to see. Don't cry, dear."

"Want to see the damned chameleon," said Archie, with his hands in his eyes. "Want father to take me to the Zoo."

"You can't go to the Zoo this time of the evening. What do you mean?"

"I want to see the damned chameleon."

"You hear!" exclaimed Bruce to Edith.

"Who taught you this language?"

"Miss Townsend taught it me."

"There! It's dreadful, Edith; he's becoming a reckless liar. Fancy her dreaming of teaching him such things! If she did, of course she must be mad, and you must send her away at once. But I'm quite sure she didn't."

"Come, Archie, you know Miss Townsend never taught you to say that. What have you got into your head?"

"Well, she didn't exactly teach me to say it—she didn't give me lessons in it—but she says it herself. She said the damned chameleon was lovely; and I want to see it. She didn't say I ought to see it. But I want to. I've been wanting to ever since. She said it at lunch to-day, and I do want to. Lots of other boys go to the Zoo, and why shouldn't I? I want to see it so much."

"Edith, I must speak to Miss Townsend about this very seriously. In the first place, people have got no right to talk about queer animals to the boy at all—we all know what he is—and in such language! I should have thought a girl like Miss Townsend, who has passed examinations in Germany, and so forth, would have had more sense of her responsibility —more tact. It shows a dreadful want of—— I hardly know what to think of it—the daughter of a clergyman, too!"

"It's all right, Bruce," Edith laughed. "Miss Townsend told me she had been to see the *Dame aux Camélias* some time ago. She was enthusiastic about it. Archie dear, I'll take you to the Zoological Gardens and we'll see lots of other animals. And don't use that expression."

"What! Can't I see the da——"

"Mr. Vincy," announced the servant.

"I must go and dress," said Bruce.

Vincy Wenham Vincy was always called by everyone simply Vincy. Applied to him it seemed like a pet name. He had arrived at the right moment, as he always did. He was very devoted to both Edith and Bruce, and he was a confidant of both. He sometimes said to Edith that he felt he was just what was wanted in the little home; an intimate stranger coming in occasionally with a fresh atmosphere was often of great value (as, for instance, now) in calming or averting storms.

Had anyone asked Vincy exactly what he was he would probably have said he was an Observer, and really he did very little else, though after he left Oxford he had taken to writing a little, and painting less. He was very fair, the fairest person one could imagine over five years old. He had pale silky hair, a minute fair moustache, very good features, a single eyeglass, and the appearance, always, of having been very recently taken out of a bandbox.

But when people fancied from this look of his that he was an empty-headed fop they soon found themselves immensely mistaken.

He was thirty-eight, but looked a gilded youth of twenty; and *was* sufficiently gilded (as he said), not perhaps exactly to be comfortable, but to enable him to get about comfortably, and see those who were.

He had a number of relatives in high places, who bored him, and were always trying to get him married. He had taken up various occupations and travelled a good deal. But his greatest pleasure was the study of people. There was nothing cold in his observation, nothing of the cynical analyst. He was impulsive, though very quiet, immensely and ardently sympathetic and almost too impressionable and enthusiastic. It was not surprising that he was immensely popular generally, as well as specially; he was so interested in everyone except himself.

No one was ever a greater general favourite.

There seemed to be no type of person on whom he jarred. People who disagreed on every other subject agreed in liking Vincy.

But he did not care in the least for acquaintances, and spent much ingenuity in trying to avoid them; he only liked intimate friends, and of all he had perhaps the Ottleys were his greatest favourites.

His affection for them dated from a summer they had spent in the same hotel in France. He had become extraordinary interested in them. He delighted in Bruce, but had with Edith, of course, more mutual understanding and intellectual sympathy, and though they met constantly, his friendship with her had never been misunderstood. Frivolous friends of his who did not know her might amuse themselves by being humorous and flippant about Vincy's little Ottleys, but no one who had ever seen them together could possibly make a mistake. They were an example of the absurdity of a tradition—"the world's" proneness to calumny. Such friendships, when genuine, are never misconstrued. Perhaps society is more often taken in the other way. But as a matter of fact the truth on this subject, as on most others, is always known in time. No one had ever even tried to explain away the intimacy, though Bruce had all the air of being unable to do without Vincy's society sometimes cynically attributed to husbands in a different position.

Vincy was pleased with the story of the Mitchells that Edith told him, and she was glad to hear that he knew the Mitchells and had been to the house.

"How like you to know everyone. What did they do?"

"The night I was there they played games," said Vincy. He spoke in a soft, even voice. "It was just a little—well—perhaps just a *tiny* bit ghastly, I thought; but don't tell Bruce. That evening I thought the people weren't quite young enough, and when they played 'Oranges and Lemons, and the Bells of St. Clements,' and so on—their bones seemed to—well, sort of rattle, if you know what I mean. But still perhaps it was only my fancy. Mitchell has such very high spirits, you see, and is determined to make everything go. He won't have conventional parties, and insists on plenty of verve; so, of course, one's forced to have it." He sighed. "They haven't any children, and they make a kind of hobby of entertaining in an unconventional way."

"It sounds rather fun. Perhaps you will be asked next Thursday. Try."

"I'll try. I'll call, and remind her of me. I

daresay she'll ask me. She's very good-natured. She believes in spiritualism, too."

"I wonder who'll be there?"

"Anyone might be there, or anyone else. As they say of marriage, it's a lottery. They might have roulette, or a spiritual séance, or Kubelik, or fancy dress heads."

"Fancy dress heads!"

"Yes. Or a cotillion, or just bridge. You never know. The house is rather like a country house, and they behave accordingly. Even hide-and-seek, I believe, sometimes. And Mitchell adores unpractical jokes, too."

"*I* see. It's rather exciting that I'm going to the Mitchells at last."

"Yes, perhaps it will be the turning-point of your life," said Vincy. "Ah! here's Bruce."

"I don't think much of that opera glass your mother gave you," Bruce remarked to his wife, soon after the curtain rose.

"It's the fashion," said Edith. "It's jade—the latest thing."

"I don't care if it is the fashion. It's no use. Here, try it, Vincy."

He handed it to Vincy, who gave Bruce a quick look, and then tried it.

"Rather quaint and pretty, I think. I like the effect," he said, handing it back to Bruce.

"It may be quaint and pretty, and it may be the latest thing, and it may be jade," said Bruce rather sarcastically, "but I'm not a slave to fashion. I never was. And I don't see any use whatever in an opera glass that makes everything look smaller instead of larger, and at a greater distance instead of nearer. I call it rot. I always say what I think. And you can tell your mother what I said if you like."

"You're looking through it the wrong side, dear," said Edith.

CHAPTER III

THE GOLDEN QUORIBUS

EDITH had been very pretty at twenty, but at twenty-eight her prettiness had immensely increased; she had really become a beauty of a particularly troubling type. She had long, deep blue eyes, clearly-cut features, hair of that soft, fine light brown just tinged with red called by the French châtain clair; and a flower-like complexion. She was slim, but not angular, and had a reposeful grace and a decided attraction for both men and women. They generally tried to express this fascination by discovering resemblances in her to various well-known pictures of celebrated artists. She had been compared to almost every type of all the great painters: Botticelli, Sir Peter Lely, Gainsborough, Burne-Jones. Some people said she was like a Sargent, others called her a post-impressionist type; there was no end to the old and new masters of whom she seemed to remind people; and she certainly had the rather insidious charm of somehow recalling the past while suggesting something undiscovered in the future. There was a good deal that was enigmatic about her. It was natural, not assumed as a pose of mysteriousness. She was not all on the surface: not obvious. One wondered. Was she capable of any depth of feeling? Was she always just sweet and tactful and clever, or could there be another side to her character? Had she (for instance) a temperament? This question was considered one of interest, so Edith had a great many admirers. Some were new and fickle, others were old and faithful. She had never yet shown more than a conversational interest in any of them, but always seemed to be laughing with a soft mockery at her own success.

Edith was not a vain woman, not even much interested in dress, though she had a quick eye and a sure impressionistic gift for it. She was always an immense favourite with women, who felt subconsciously grateful to her for her wonderful forbearance. To have the power and not to use it! To be so pretty, yet never *to take anyone away!*—not even coldly to display her conquests. But this liking she did not, as a rule, return in any decided fashion. She had dreadfully little to say to the average woman, except to a few intimate friends, and frankly preferred the society of the average man, although she had not as yet developed a taste for coquetry, for which she had, however, many natural gifts. She was much taken up by Bruce, by Archie and Dilly, and was fond of losing herself in ideas and in books, and in various artistic movements and fads in which her interest was cultivated and perhaps inspired by Vincy. Vincy was her greatest friend and confidant. He was really a great safety-valve, and she told him nearly every thought.

Still, Archie was, so far, her greatest interest. He was a particularly pretty boy, and she was justified in thinking him rather unusual. At this period he spent a considerable amount of his leisure time not only in longing to see real animals, but in inventing and drawing pictures of non-existent ones—horrible creatures, or quaint creatures, for which he found the strangest names. He told Dilly about them, but Dilly was not his audience—she was rather his confidante and literary adviser; or even sometimes his collaborator. His public consisted principally of his mother. It was a convention that Edith should be frightened, shocked and horrified at the creatures of his imagination, while Dilly privately revelled in their success. Mi s Townsend, the governess, was rather coldly ignored in this matter. She had a way of speaking of the animals with a smile, as a nice occupation to keep the children quiet. She did not understand.

"Please, madam, would you kindly go into the nursery; Master Archie wishes you to come and hear about the golden—something he's just made up like," said Dilly's nurse with an expression of resignation.

Edith jumped up at once.

"Oh dear! Tell Master Archie I'm coming."

She ran into the nursery and found Archie and Dilly both looking rather excited; Archie, fairly self-controlled, with a paper in his hand on which was a rough sketch which he would not let her see, and hid behind him.

"Mother," Archie began in a low, solemn voice, rather slowly, "the golden quoribus is the most horrible animal, the most awful-*looking* animal, you ever heard of in *your* life!"

"Oh-h-h! How awful!" said Edith, beginning to shiver. "Wait a moment—let me sit down quietly and hear about it."

She sat down by the fire and clasped her hands, looking at him with a terrified expression which was part of the ritual.

Dilly giggled, and put her thumb in her

mouth, watching the effect with widely opened eyes.

"Much more awful than the gazeka, of course, I suppose?" Edith said rather rashly.

"Much," said Dilly.

"(Be quiet, Dilly!) Mother!" he was reproachful, "what do you mean? The gazeka? Why—the gazeka's nothing at all—it's a rotten little animal. It doesn't count. Besides, it isn't real—it never was real. Gazeka, indeed!"

"Oh, I beg your pardon," said Edith repentantly; "do go on."

"No . . . the golden quoribus is far-ar-r-r-r more frightening even than the jilbery. Do you remember how awful *that* was? And much larger."

"What! Worse than the jilbery! Oh, good gracious! How dreadful! What's it like?"

"First of all—it's as long as from here to Brighton," said Archie.

"A little longer," said Dilly.

"(Shut up, miss!) *As* long. It's called the golden quoribus because it's bright gold, except the bumps; and the bumps are green."

"Bright green," said Dilly.

"(Oh, will you hold your tongue, Dilly?) Green."

"How terrible! . . . And what shape is it?"

"All pointed and sharp, and three-cornered."

"Does it breathe fire?" asked Edith.

Archie smiled contemptuously.

"Breathe fire! Oh, mother! Do you think it's a silly dragon in a fairy story? Of course it doesn't. How can it breathe fire?"

"Sorry," said Edith apologetically. "Go on."

"*But*, the peculiar thing about it, besides that it lives entirely on muffins and mutton, and the frightening part, I'm coming to now." He became emphatic, and spoke slowly. "The golden quoribus has more claws than any . . . other . . . animal . . . in the whole world!"

"Oh-h-h," she shuddered.

"Yes," said Archie solemnly. "It has large claws coming out of its head."

"Its head! Good gracious!"

"It has claws here and claws there; claws coming out of the eyes; and claws coming out of the ears; and claws coming out of its shoulders; and claws coming out of the forehead!"

Edith shivered with fright and held up her hands in front of her eyes to ward off the picture.

"And claws coming out of the mouth," said Archie, coming a step nearer to her and raising his voice.

Edith jumped.

"And claws coming out of the hands, and claws coming out of the feet!"

"Yes," said Dilly, wildly and recklessly and jumping up and down, "and claws on the ceiling, and claws on the floor, and claws all over the world!"

With one violent slap she was sent sprawling.

Shrieks, sobs and tears filled the quiet nursery.

"I know," said Archie, when he had been persuaded to apologise, "of course I know a gentleman oughtn't to hit a lady, not even—I mean, especially not if she's his little sister. But oh, mother, *ought* a lady to interrupt a story?"

When Edith told Vincy he entirely took Archie's side.

Suppose Sargent were painting a beautiful picture, and one of his pupils, snatching the paint-brush from him, insisted on finishing it, and spoiling it—how would *he* like it? Imagine a poet who had just written a great poem, and been interrupted in reciting it by someone who quickly finished it off all wrong! The author might be forgiven under such circumstances if in his irritation he took a strong line. In Vincy's opinion it served Dilly jolly well right. Young?

Of course she was young, but four (he said) was not a day too soon to begin to learn to respect the work of the artist. Edith owned that Archie was not easily exasperated, and was as a rule very patient with the child. Bruce took an entirely different view. He was quite gloomy about it and feared that Archie showed every sign of growing up to be an Apache.

CHAPTER IV

THE MITCHELLS

THE Mitchells were, as Vincy had said, extremely hospitable; they had a perfect mania for receiving; they practically lived for it, and the big house at Hampstead, with its large garden covered in, and a sort of studio built out, was scarcely ever without guests. When they didn't have some sort of party they invariably went out.

Mitchell's great joy was to make his parties different from others by some childish fantasy or other. He especially delighted in a surprise. He often took the trouble (for instance) to have a telegram sent to every one of his guests during the course of the evening. Each of these wires contained some personal chaff or practical joke. At other times he would give everyone little presents, concealed in some way. Christmas didn't come once a year to the Mitchells; it seemed never to go away. One was always surprised not to find a Christmas tree and crackers. These entertainments, always splendidly done materially, and curiously erratic socially, were sometimes extremely amusing; at others, of course, a frost; it was rather a toss-up.

And the guests were, without exception, the most extraordinary mixture in London. They included delightful people, absurd people, average people; people who were smart and people who were dowdy, some who were respectable and nothing else, some who were deplorable, others beautiful, and many merely dull. There was never the slightest attempt at any sort of harmonising, or of suitability; there was a great deal of kindness to the hard-up, and a wild and extravagant delight in any novelty. In fact, the Mitchells were everything except exclusive, and as they were not guided by any sort of rule, they really lived, in St. John's Wood, superior to suburban or indeed any other restrictions. They would ask the same guests to dinner time after time, six or seven times in succession. They would invite cordially a person of no attraction whatsoever whom they had only just met, and they would behave with casual coolness to desirable acquaintances or favourite friends whom they had known all their lives. However, there was no doubt that their parties had got the name for being funny, and that was quite enough. London people in every set are so desperate for something out of the ordinary way, for variety and oddness, that the Mitchells were frequently asked for invitations by most distinguished persons who hoped, in their *blasé* fatigue, to meet something new and queer.

For the real Londoner is a good deal of a child, and loves Punch and Judy shows, and conjuring tricks (symbolically speaking)—and is also often dreaming of the chance of meeting some spring novelty, in the way of a romance. Although the Mitchells were proud of these successes they were as free from snobbishness as almost anyone could be. On the whole Mrs. Mitchell had a slight weakness for celebrities, while Mr. Mitchell preferred pretty women, or people who romped. It was merely from carelessness that the Ottleys had never been asked before.

When Edith and Bruce found themselves in the large square country-house-looking hall, with its oak beams and early English fireplace, about twenty people had arrived, and as many more were expected. A lively chatter had already begun; for each woman had been offered on her arrival a basket from which she had to choose a brightly coloured ribbon. These ribbons matched the rosettes presented in an equally haphazard way to every man. As Vincy observed, it gave one the rather ghastly impression that there was going to be a cotillion at once, on sight, before dinner; which was a little frightening. In reality it was merely so that the partners for the meal should be chosen by chance. Mitchell thought this more fun than arranging guests; but there was an element of gambling about it that made wary people nervous. Everyone present would have cheated had it been possible. But it was not.

Mrs. Mitchell was a tiny brown-eyed creature, who looked absurdly young; she was kind, sprightly, and rather like a grouse. Mitchell was a jovial-looking man, with a high forehead, almost too much ease of manner, and a twinkling eye.

The chief guests to-night consisted of Lord Rye, a middle-aged suffraget, who was known for his habit of barking before he spoke and for his wonderful ear for music—he could play all Richard, Oscar and Johann Strauss's compositions by ear on the piano, and never mixed them up; Aylmer Ross, the handsome barrister; Myra Mooney, who had been on the stage; and an intelligent foreigner from the embassy, with a decoration, a goat-like beard, and an Armenian accent. Mrs. Mitchell said he was the minister from some place with a name like Ruritania.

She had a vague memory. There was also a Mr. Cricker, a very young man of whom it was said that he could dance like Nijinsky, but never would; and the rest were chiefly Foreign Office clerks (like Mitchell and Bruce), more barristers and their wives, a soldier or two, some undergraduates, a lady photographer, a few pretty girls, and vague people. There were to be forty guests for dinner and a few more in the evening.

Almost immediately on her arrival Edith noticed a tall, clean-shaven man, with smooth fair hair, observant blue eyes, and a rather humorous expression, and she instantly decided that she would try to will him to take her to dinner. (Rather a superfluous effort of magnetism, since it must have been settled already by fate and the ribbons.) It was obvious from one quick glance that he shared the wish. To their absurdly great mutual disappointment (a lot of ground was covered very quickly at the Mitchells), their ribbons didn't match, and she was taken to dinner by Captain Willis, who looked dull. Fortune, however, favoured her. On her other side she found the man who looked amusing. He was introduced to her across the table by Mrs. Mitchell, with *empressement*, as Mr. Aylmer Ross.

Edith felt happy to-night; her spirits were raised by what she felt to be an atmosphere *tiède*, as the French say; full of indulgence, sympathetic, relaxing, in which either cleverness or stupidity could float equally at its ease. The puerility of the silly little arrangements to amuse removed all sense of ceremony. The note is always struck by the hostess, and she was everything that was amiable, without effort or affectation.

No one was ever afraid of her.

Bruce's neighbour at dinner was the delicate, battered-looking actress, in a Royal fringe and a tight bodice with short sleeves, who had once been a celebrity, though no one remembered for what. Miss Myra Mooney, formerly a beauty, had known her days of success. She had been the supreme performer of ladylike parts. She had been known as the very quintessence of refinement. It was assumed when she first came out that a duke would go to the devil for her in her youth, and that in her late maturity she would tour the provinces with *The Three Musketeers*. Neither of these prophecies had, however, been fulfilled. She still occasionally took small middle-aged titled parts in repertoire matinees. She was unable to help referring constantly to the hit she made in *Peril* at Manchester in 1887; nor could she ever resist speaking of the young man who sent her red carnations every day of his blighted existence for fifteen years; a pure romance, indeed, for, as she owned, he never even wished to be introduced to her. She still called him poor boy, oblivious of the fact that he was now sixty-eight, and, according to the illustrated papers, spent his entire time in giving away a numberless succession of daughters in brilliant marriage at St. George's, Hanover Square.

In this way Miss Mooney lived a good deal in the past, but she was not unaware of the present, and was always particularly nice to people generally regarded as bores. So she was never without plenty of invitations. Mitchell had had formerly a slight *tendre* for her, and in his good nature pretended to think she had not altered a bit. She was still refined *comme cela ne se fait plus*; it was practically no longer possible to find such a perfect lady, even on the stage. As she also had all the easy good nature of the artist, and made herself extremely agreeable, Bruce was delighted with her, and evidently thought he had drawn a prize.

"I wondered," Aylmer Ross said, "whether this could possibly happen. First I half hoped it might; then I gave it up in despair."

"So did I," said Edith; "and yet I generally

know. I've a touch of second sight, I think—at dinner-parties."

"Oh, well, I have second sight too—any amount; only it's always wrong. However! ..."

"Aren't the Mitchells dears?" said Edith.

"Oh, quite. Do you know them well?"

"Very well, indeed. But I've never seen them before."

"Ah, I see. Well, now we've found our way here—broken the ice and that sort of thing—we must often come and dine with them, mustn't we, Mrs. Ottley? Can't we come again next week?"

"Very sweet of you to ask us, I'm sure."

"Not at all; very jolly of us to turn up. The boot is on the other leg, or whatever the phrase is. By the way, I'm sure you know everything, Mrs. Ottley, tell me, did people ever wear only one boot at a time, do you think, or how did this expression originate?"

"I wonder."

Something in his suave manner of taking everything for granted seemed to make them know each other almost too quickly, and gave her an odd sort of self-consciousness. She turned to Captain Willis on her other side.

"I say," he said querulously, "isn't this a bit off? We've got the same coloured ribbons and you haven't said a word to me yet! Rather rot, isn't it, what?"

"Oh, haven't I? I will now."

Captain Willis lowered his voice to a confidential tone and said:

"Do you know, what I always say is—live and let live and let it go at that; what?"

"That's a dark saying," said Edith.

"Have a burnt almond," said Captain Willis inconsequently, as though it would help her to understand. "Yes, Mrs. Ottley, that's what I always say.... But people won't, you know —they won't—and there it is." He seemed resigned. "Good chap, Mitchell, isn't he? Musical chairs, I believe—that's what we're to play this evening; or bridge, whichever we like. I shall go in for bridge. I'm not musical."

"And which shall you do?" asked Aylmer of Edith. He had evidently been listening.

"Neither."

"We'll talk then, shall we? I can't play bridge either.... Mrs. Ottley—which is your husband? I didn't notice when you came in."

"Over there, opposite; the left-hand corner."

"Good-looking chap with the light moustache —next to Myra Mooney?"

"That's it," she said. "He seems to be enjoying himself. I'm glad he's got Miss Mooney. He's lucky."

"He is indeed," said Aylmer.

"She's a wonderful-looking woman—like an old photograph, or someone in a book," said Edith.

"Do you care for books?"

"Oh, yes, rather. I've just been discovering Bourget. Fancy, I didn't know about him! I've just read 'Mensonges' for the first time."

"Oh yes. Rather a pompous chap, isn't he? But you could do worse than read 'Mensonges' for the first time."

"I *have* done worse. I've been reading Rudyard Kipling for the last time."

"Really! Don't you like him? Why?"

"I feel all the time, somehow, as if he were calling me by my Christian name without an introduction, or as if he wanted me to exchange hats with him," she said. "He's so fearfully familiar with his readers."

"But you think he keeps at a respectful distance from his characters? However—why worry about books at all, Mrs. Ottley? Flowers, lilies of the field, and so forth, don't toil or spin; why should they belong to libraries? I don't think you ever ought to read—except perhaps sometimes a little poetry, or romance. . . . You see, that is what you are, rather, isn't it?"

"Don't you care for books?" she answered,

ignoring the compliment. "I should have thought you loved them, and knew everything about them. I'm not sure that I know."

"You know quite enough, believe me," he answered earnest'y. "Oh, don't be cultured—don't talk about Lloyd George! Don't take an intelligent interest in the subjects of the day!"

"All right; I'll try not."

She turned with a laugh to Captain Willis, who seemed very depressed.

"I say, you know," he said complainingly, "this is all very well. It's all very well no doubt. But I only ask one thing—just one. Is this cricket? I merely ask, you know. Just that—is it cricket; what?"

"It isn't meant to be. What's the matter?"

"Why, I'm simply fed up and broken-hearted, you know. Hardly two words have I had with you to-night, Mrs. Ottley. . . . I suppose that chap's awfully amusing, what? I'm not amusing. . . . I know that."

"Oh, don't say that. Indeed you are," she consoled him.

"Am I though?"

"Well, you amuse *me*!"

"Right!" He laughed cheerily. He always filled up pauses with a laugh.

CHAPTER V

THE SURPRISE

CERTAINLY Mrs. Mitchell on one side and Captain Willis on the other had suffered neglect. But they seemed to become hardened to it towards the end of dinner. . . .

"I have a boy, too," Aylmer remarked irrelevantly, "rather a nice chap. Just ten."

Though only by the merest, slightest movement of an eyelash Edith could not avoid showing her surprise. No one ever had less the air of a married man. Also, she was quite ridiculously disappointed. One can't say why, but one doesn't talk to a married man quite in the same way or so frankly as to a bachelor—if one is a married woman. She did not ask about his wife, but said:

"Fancy! Boys are rather nice things to have about, aren't they?"

She was looking round the table, trying to divine which was Mrs. Aylmer Ross. No, she wasn't there. Edith felt sure of it. It was an unaccountable satisfaction.

"Yes; he's all right. And now give me a detailed description of *your* children."

"I can't. I never could talk about them."

"I see.... I should like to see them.... I saw you speak to Vincy. Dear little fellow, isn't he?"

"He's a great friend of mine."

"I'm tremendously devoted to him, too. He's what used to be called an exquisite. And he *is* exquisite; he has an exquisite mind. But, of course, you know what a good sort he is."

"Rather."

"He seems rather to look at life than to act in it, doesn't he?" continued Aylmer. "He's a brilliant sort of spectator. Vincy thinks that all the world's a stage, but *he's* always in the front row of the stalls. I never could be like that.... I always want to be right in the thick of it, on in every scene, and always performing!"

"To an audience?" said Edith.

He smiled and went on.

"What's so jolly about him is that though he's so quiet, yet he's genial; not chilly and reserved. He's frank, I mean—and confiding. Without ever saying much. He expresses himself in his own way."

"That's quite true."

"And, after all, it's really only expression that makes things real. 'If you don't talk about a thing, it has never happened.'"

"But it doesn't always follow that a thing has happened because you do talk about it," said Edith. "Ah, Mrs. Mitchell's going!"

She floated away.

He remained in a rather ecstatic state of absence of mind.

Mrs. Mitchell gladly told Edith all about Aylmer Ross, how clever he was, how nice, how devoted to his little boy. He had married very young, it seemed, and had lost his wife two years after. This was ten years ago, and according to Mrs. Mitchell he had never looked at another woman since. Women love to simplify in this sentimental way.

"However," said she consolingly, "he's still quite young, under forty, and he's sure to fall in love and marry again."

"No doubt," said Edith, wishing the first wife had remained alive. She disliked the non-existent second one.

Nearly all the men had now joined the ladies in the studio, with the exception of Bruce and of Aylmer Ross. Mrs. Mitchell had taken an immense fancy to Edith and showed it by telling her all about a wonderful little tailor who made coats and skirts better than Lucile for next to nothing, and by introducing to her Lord Rye and the embassy man, and Mr. Cricker. Edith was sitting in a becoming corner under a shaded light from which she could watch the door, when Vincy came up to talk to her.

"You seemed to get on rather well at dinner," he said.

"Yes; isn't Captain Willis a dear?"

"Oh, simply sweet. So bright and clever. I was sure you'd like him, Edith."

Captain Willis here came up and said, a shade more jovially than he had spoken at dinner, with his laugh:

"Well, you know, Mrs. Ottley, what I always say is—live and let live and let it go at that; what? But they never *do*, you know! They won't—and there it is!"

Edith now did a thing she had never done in her life before and which was entirely unlike her. She tried her utmost to retain the group round her, and to hold their attention. For a reason of which she was hardly conscious, she wanted Aylmer Ross to see her surrounded. The minister from the place with a name like Ruritania was so immensely bowled over that he was already murmuring in a low voice (almost a hiss, as they say in melodrama): "*Vous êtes chez vous, quand? Dites un mot, un mot seulement, et je me précipiterai à vos pieds,*" while at the same time, in her other ear, Lord Rye was explaining (to her pretended intense interest) how he could play the whole of *Elektra*, *The Chocolate Soldier* and *Nightbirds* by ear without a single mistake. ("Perfectly sound!" grumbled Captain Willis, "but why do it?") Vincy was listening, enjoying himself. Bruce came in at last, evidently engaged in an absorbed and intimate conversation with Aylmer Ross. They seemed so much interested in their talk that they went to the other end of the room and sat down there together. Aylmer gave her one glance only.

Edith was unreasonably annoyed. What on earth could he and Bruce find to talk about? At length, growing tired of her position, she got up, and walked across the room to look at a picture on the wall, turning her graceful back to the room.

Bruce had now at last left his companion, but still Aylmer Ross did not go and speak to her, though he was sitting alone.

Musical chairs began in the studio. Someone was playing "Baby, look-a-here," stopping suddenly in the middle to shouts of laughter and shrieks from the romping players. In the drawing-room some of the people were playing bridge. How dull the rest of the evening was! Just before the party practically broke up, Edith had an opportunity of saying as she passed Aylmer:

"I thought we were going to have a talk instead of playing games?"

"I saw you were occupied," he answered ceremoniously. "I didn't like—to interrupt."

She laughed. "Is this a jealous scene, Mr. Ross?"

"I wonder," he said, smiling, "and if so, whose. Well, I hope to see you again soon."

"*What* a success your charming wife has had to-night," said Mrs. Mitchell to Bruce, as they took leave. "Everyone is quite wild about her. How pretty she is! You *must* be proud of her."

They were nearly the last. Mr. Cricker, who had firmly refused the whole evening, in spite of abject entreaties, to dance like Nijinsky, suddenly relented when everyone had forgotten all about it, and was leaping alone in the studio, while Lord Rye, always a great lingerer, was playing Richard Strauss to himself on the baby Grand, and moking a huge cigar.

"Edith," said Bruce solemnly, as they drove away, "I've made a friend to-night. There was one really charming man there—he took an immense fancy to me."

"Oh—who was that?"

"Who was that?" he mimicked her, but quite good-naturedly. "How stupid women are in some things! Why, Aylmer Ross, the chap who sat next to you at dinner! I suppose you didn't appreciate him. Very clever, very interesting. He was anxious to know several things which I was glad to be in a position to tell him. Yes—an awfully good sort. I asked him to dine at my club one day, to go on with our conversation."

"Oh, did you?"

"Yes. Why shouldn't I? However, it seems from what he said that he thinks the Carlton's nicer for a talk, so I'm going to ask him there instead. You can come too, dear. He won't mind; it won't prevent our talking "

"Oh, are we going to give a dinner at the Carlton?"

"I wish you wouldn't oppose me, Edith. Once in a way! Of course I shall. Our flat's too small to give a decent dinner. He's one of the nicest chaps I've ever met."

"Well, do you want me to write to-morrow morning then, dear?"

"Er—no—I have asked him already."

"Oh, really—which day?"

"Well, I *suggested* next Thursday—but he thought to-morrow would be better; he's engaged for every other day. Now don't go and say you're engaged to-morrow. If you are, you'll have to chuck it!"

"Oh no; I'm not engaged."

Mentally rearranging her evening dress, Edith drove home thoughtfully. She was attracted and did not know why, and for the first time hoped she had made an impression. It had been a long evening, and her headache, she said, necessitated solitude and darkness at once.

"All right. I've got a much worse headache —gout, I think, but never mind about me. Don't be anxious, dear! I say, that Miss Mooney is a very charming woman. She took rather a fancy to me, Edith. Er—you might ask her to dinner too, if you like, to make a fourth!"

"But—really! Ought we to snatch all the Mitchells' friends the first time, Bruce?"

"Why, of course, it's only courteous. It's all right. One must return their hospitality."

CHAPTER VI

THE VISIT

THE following afternoon Edith was standing by the piano in her condensed white drawing-room, trying over a song, which she was accompanying with one hand, when to her surprise the maid announced "Mr. Aylmer Ross." It was a warm day, and though there was a fire the windows were open, letting in the scent of the mauve and pink hyacinths in the little window-boxes. She thought as she came forward to meet him that he seemed entirely different from last night. Her first impression was that he was too big for the room, her second that he was very handsome, and also a little agitated.

"I really hardly know how to apologise, Mrs. Ottley. I oughtn't to have turned up in this cool way. But your husband has kindly asked me to dine with you to-night, and I wasn't sure of the time. I thought I'd come and ask you." He waited a minute. "Of course, if I hadn't been so fortunate as to find you in, I should just have left a note." He looked round the room.

Obviously it was quite unnecssary for him to have called; he could have sent the note that he had brought with him. She was flattered. She thought that she liked his voice and the flash of his white teeth when he smiled.

"Oh, I'm glad I'm at home," she said, in a gentle way that put him at his ease, and yet at an immense distance. "I felt in the mood to stop at home and play the piano to-day. I'm delighted to see you." They sat down by the fire. "It's at eight to-night. Shall we have tea?"

"Oh no, thanks; isn't it too early? I sha'n't keep you a moment. Thanks very much. . . . You were playing something when I came in. I wish you'd play it to me over again."

Nine women out of ten would have refused, saying they knew nothing of music, or that they were out of practice, or that they never played except for their own amusement, or something of the kind; especially if they took no pride whatever in that accomplishment. But Edith went back to the piano at once, and went on trying over the song that she didn't know, without making any excuse for the faltering notes.

"That's charming," he said. "Thanks. Tosti, of course."

She came back to the fireplace. "Of course. We had great fun last night, didn't we?"

"Oh, *I* enjoyed myself immensely; part of the time at least."

"But after dinner you were rather horrid, Mr. Ross. You wouldn't come and talk to me, would you?"

"Wouldn't I? I was afraid. Tell me, do I seem many years older since last night?" he asked.

"I don't see any difference. Why?"

"Because I've lived months—almost years—since I saw you last. Time doesn't go by hours, does it? . . . What a charming little room this is. It suits you. There's hardly anything in it, but everything is right."

"I don't like to have many things in a room," said Edith, holding out her delicate hands to the fire. "It makes me nervous. I have gradually accustomed Bruce to my idea by removing one thing at a time—photographs, pictures, horrid old wedding presents, all the little things people have. They suggest too many different trains of thought. They worry me. He's getting used to it now. He says, soon there'll be nothing left but a couple of chairs and a bookcase!"

"And how right! I've had rather the same idea in my house, but I couldn't keep it up. It's different for a man alone; things seem to accumulate; especially pictures. I know such a lot of artists. I'm very unfortunate in that respect. ... I really feel I oughtn't to have turned up like this, Mrs. Ottley."

"Why not?"

"You're very kind. ... Excuse my country manners, but how nice your husband is. He was very kind to me."

"He liked *you* very much, too."

"He seems charming," he repeated, then said with a change of tone and with his occasional impulsive brusqueness, "I wonder—does he ever jar on you in any way?"

"Oh no. Never. He couldn't. He amuses me," Edith replied softly.

"Oh, does he? ... If I had the opportunity I wonder if I should *amuse* you," he spoke thoughtfully.

"No; I don't think you would at all," said Edith, looking him straight in the face.

"That's quite fair," he laughed, and seemed rather pleased. "You mean I should bore you to death! Do forgive me, Mrs. Ottley. Let's go on with our talk of last night. ... I feel it's rather like the Palace of Truth here; I don't know why. There must be something in the atmosphere—I seem to find it difficult not to think aloud—Vincy, now—do you see much of Vincy?"

"Oh yes; he comes here most days, or we talk on the telephone."

"I see; he's your confidant, and you're his. Dear Vincy. By the way, he asked me last night to go to a tea-party at his flat next week. He was going to ask one or two other kindred spirits—as I think they're called. To see something—some collection. Including you, of course?"

"I shall certainly go," said Edith, "whether he asks me or not."

Aylmer seemed to be trying to leave. He nearly got up once or twice and sat down again.

"Well, I shall see you to-night," he said. "At eight."

"Yes."

"What shall you wear, Mrs. Ottley?"

"Oh, I thought, perhaps, my mauve chiffon? What do you advise?" she smiled.

"Not what you wore last night?"

"Oh no."

"It was very jolly. I liked it. Er—red, wasn't it?"

"Oh *no!* It was pink!" she answered.

Then there was an extraordinary pause, in which neither of them seemed able to think of anything to say. There was a curious sort of vibration in the air.

"Isn't it getting quite springy?" said Edith, as she glanced at the window. "It's one of those sort of warm days that seem to have got mixed up by mistake with the winter."

"Very," was his reply, which was not very relevant.

Another pause was beginning.

"Mr. Vincy," announced the servant.

He was received with enthusiasm, and Aylmer Ross now recovered his ease and soon went away.

"Edith!" said Vincy, in a reproving tone. "*Really!* How *very* soon!"

"He came to know what time we dine. He was just passing."

"Oh yes. He would want to know. He lives in Jermyn Street. I suppose Knightsbridge is on his way to there."

"From where?" she asked.

"From here," said Vincy.

"What happened after we left?" said Edith.

"I saw the Cricker man beginning to dance with hardly anyone looking at him."

"Isn't his imitation of Nijinsky wonderful?" asked Vincy.

"Simply marvellous! I thought he was imitating George Grossmith. Do you know, I love the Mitchells, Vincy. It's really great fun there. Fancy, Bruce seems so delighted with Aylmer Ross and Miss Mooney that he insisted on their both dining with us to-night."

"He seemed rather carried away, I thought. There's a fascination about Aylmer. There are so many things he's not," said Vincy.

"Tell me some of them."

"Well, for one thing, he's not fatuous, though he's so good-looking. He's not a lady-killing sort of person or anything else tedious."

She was delighted at this especially.

"If he took a fancy to a person—well, it might be rather serious, if you take my meaning," said Vincy.

"How sweet of him! So unusual. Do you like Myra Mooney?"

"Me? Oh, rather; I'm devoted to her. She's a delightful type. Get her on to the subject of the red carnations. She's splendid about them. . . . She received them every day at breakfast-time for fifteen years. Another jolly thing about Aylmer is that he has none of that awful old-fashioned modernness, thank goodness!"

"Ah, I noticed that."

THE VISIT

"I suppose he wasn't brilliant to-day. He was too thrilled. But, do be just a teeny bit careful, Edith dear, because when he is at all he's very much so. Do you see?"

"What a lot you seem to think of one little visit, Vincy! After all, it was only one."

"There hasn't been time yet for many more, has there, Edith dear? He could hardly call twice the same day, on the first day, too ... Yes, I come over quite queer and you might have knocked me down with a feather, in a manner of speaking, when I clapped eyes on him setting here."

Edith liked Vincy to talk in his favourite Cockney strain. It contrasted pleasantly with his soft, even voice and *raffiné* appearance.

"Here's Bruce," she said.

Bruce came in carrying an enormous basket of gilded straw. It was filled with white heather, violets, lilies, jonquils, gardenias and mimosa. The handle was trimmed with mauve ribbon.

"Oh, Bruce! How angelic of you!"

"Don't be in such a hurry, dear. These are not from me. They arrived just at the same time that I did. Brought by a commissionaire. There was hardly room for it in the lift."

Edith looked quickly at the card. It bore the name of the minister of the place with a name like Ruritania.

"What cheek!" exclaimed Bruce, who was really flattered. "What infernal impertinence. Upon my word I've more than half a mind to go and tell him what I think of him—straight from the shoulder. *What's* the address?"

"Grosvenor Square."

"Well, I don't care. I shall go straight to the embassy," said Bruce. "No, I sha'n't. I'll send them back and write him a line—tell him that Englishwomen are not in the habit of accepting presents from undesirable aliens. ... I consider it a great liberty. Aren't I right, Vincy?"

"Quite. But perhaps he means no harm, Bruce. I daresay it's the custom in the place with the funny name. You see, you never know, in a place like that."

"Then you don't think I ought to take it up?"

"I don't want them. It's a very oppressive basket," Edith said.

"How like you, Edith! I thought you were fond of flowers."

"So I am, but I like one at a time. This is too miscellaneous and crowded."

"Some women are never satisfied. It's very rude and ungrateful to the poor old man, who meant to be nice, no doubt, and to show his respect for Englishwomen. I think you ought to write and thank him," said Bruce. "And let me see the letter before it goes."

CHAPTER VII

COUP DE FOUDRE

WHEN Aylmer Ross got back to the little brown house in Jermyn Street he went to his library, and took from a certain drawer an ivory miniature framed in black. He looked at it for some time. It had a sweet, old-fashioned face, with a very high forehead, blue eyes, and dark hair arranged in two festoons of plaits, turned up at the sides. It represented his mother in the early sixties, and he thought it was like Edith. He had a great devotion and cult for the memory of his mother. When he was charmed with a woman he always imagined her to be like his mother.

He had never thought this about his wife. People had said how extraordinarily Aylmer must have been in love to have married that uninteresting girl, no one in particular, not pretty and a little second-rate. As a matter of fact the marriage had happened entirely by accident. It had occurred through a misunderstanding during a game of consequences in a country house. She was terribly literal. Having taken some joke of his seriously, she had sent him a touchingly coy letter, saying she was overwhelmed at his offer (feeling she was hardly worthy to be his wife) and must think it over. He did not like to hurt her feelings by explaining, and when she relented and accepted him he couldn't bear to tell her the truth. He was absurdly tender-hearted, and he thought that, after all, it didn't matter so very much. The little house left him by his mother needed a mistress; he would probably marry somebody or other, anyhow; and she seemed such a harmless little thing. It would please her so much! When the hurried marriage had come to a pathetic end by her early death everyone was tragic about it except Aylmer. All his friends declared he was heart-broken and lonely and would never marry again. He had indeed been shocked and grieved at her death, but only for her—not at being left alone. That part was a relief. The poor little late Mrs. Aylmer Ross had turned out a terrible mistake. She had said the wrong thing from morning till night, and, combining a prim, refined manner with a vulgar point of view, had been in every way dreadfully impossible. He had really been patience and unselfishness itself to her, but he had suffered. The fact was, he had never even liked her. That was the reason he had not married again.

But he was devoted to his boy in a quiet way. He was the sort of man who is adored by children, animals, servants and women. Tall, strong and handsome, with intelligence beyond the average, yet with nothing alarming about him, good-humoured about trifles, jealous in matters of love—perhaps that is, after all, the type women really like best. It is sheer nonsense to say that women enjoy being tyrannised over. No doubt there are some who would rather be bullied than ignored. But the hectoring man is, with few exceptions, secretly detested. In so far as one can generalise (always a dangerous thing to do) it may be said that women like best a kind, clever man who can be always trusted; and occasionally (if necessary) deceived.

Aylmer hardly ever got angry except in an argument about ideas. Yet his feelings were violent; he was impulsive, and under his suave and easy-going manner emotional. He was certainly good-looking, but had he not been he would have pleased all the same. He seemed to radiate warmth, life, a certain careless good-humour. To be near him was like warming one's hands at a warm fire. Superficially susceptible and inclined to be experimental he had not the instinct of the collector and was devoid of fatuousness. But he could have had more genuine successes than all the Don Juans and Romeos and Fausts who ever climbed rope ladders. Besides his physical attraction he inspired a feeling of reliance. Women felt safe with him; he would never treat anyone badly. He inspired that kind of trust enormously in men also, and his house was constantly filled with people asking his advice and begging him to do things—sometimes not very easy ones. He was always being left guardian to young persons who would never require one, and said himself he had become almost a professional trustee.

As Aylmer was generous and very extravagant in a way of his own (though he cared nothing for show), he really worked hard at the bar to add to his already large income. He always wanted a great deal of money. He required ease, margin and elbow-room. He had no special hobbies, but he needed luxury in general of a kind, and especially the luxury of getting things in a hurry, his theory being that everything comes to the man who won't wait. He was not above detesting little material hardships. He was not the sort of man, for instance, even in his youngest days, who would go by omnibus to the gallery to the opera, to hear a favourite singer or a special performance; not that he had the faintest tinge of snobbishness, but simply because such trifling drawbacks irritated him, and spoilt his pleasure.

Impressionistic as he was in life, on the other hand, curiously, Aylmer's real taste in art and decoration was Pre-Raphaelite; delicate, detailed and meticulous almost to preciousness. He often had delightful things in his house, but never for long. He had no pleasure in property; valuable possessions worried him, and after any amount of trouble to get some object of art he would often give it away the next week. For he really liked money only for freedom and ease. The general look of the house was, consequently, distinguished, sincere and extremely comfortable. It was neither hackneyed nor bizarre, and, while it contained some interesting things, had no superfluities.

Aylmer had been spoilt as a boy and was still wilful and a little impatient. For instance he could never wait even for a boy-messenger, but always sent his notes by taxi to wait for an answer. And now he wanted something in a hurry, and was very much afraid he would never get it.

Aylmer was, as I have said, often a little susceptible. This time he felt completely bowled over. He had only seen her twice. That made no difference.

The truth was—it sounds romantic, but is really scientific, all romance being, perhaps, based on science—that Edith's appearance corresponded in every particular with an ideal that had grown up with him. Whether he had seen some picture as a child that had left a vague and lasting impression, or whatever the reason was, the moment he saw her he felt, with a curious mental sensation, as of something that fell into its place with a click ("Ça y est!"), that she realised some half-forgotten dream. In fact, it was a rare and genuine case of *coup de foudre*. Had she been a girl he would have proposed to her the next day, and they might quite possibly have married in a month, and lived happily ever after. These things occasionally happen. But she was married already.

Had she been a fool, or a bore, a silly little idiot or a fisher of men, a social sham who prattled of duchesses or a strenuous feminine politician who babbled of votes; a Christian Scientist bent on converting, an adventuress without adventures (the worst kind), a mind-healer or a body-snatcher, a hockey-player or

COUP DE FOUDRE 75

even a lady novelist, it would have been exactly the same; whatever she had been, mentally or morally, he would undoubtedly have fallen in love with her physically, at first sight. But it was very much worse than that. He found her delightful, and clever; he was certain she was an angel. She was married to Ottley. Ottley was all right. . . . Rather an ass . . . rather ridiculous; apparently in every way but one.

So absurdly hard hit was Aylmer that it seemed to him as if to see her again as soon as possible was already the sole object in his life. Did she like him? Intuitively he felt that during his little visit his intense feeling had radiated, and not displeased—perhaps a little impressed—her. He could easily, he knew, form a friendship with them; arrange to see her often. He was going to meet her to-night, through his own arrangement. He would get them to come and dine with him soon—no, the next day.

What was the good?

Well, where was the harm?

Aylmer had about the same code of morals as the best of his numerous friends in Bohemia, in clubland and in social London. He was no more scrupulous on most subjects than the ordinary man of his own class. Still, *he had been married himself.* That made an immense difference, for he was positively capable of seeing (and with sympathy) from the husband's point of view. Even now, indifferent as he had been to his own wife, and after ten years, it would have caused him pain and fury had he found out that she had ever tried to play him false. Of course, cases varied. He knew that if Edith had been free his one thought would have been to marry her. Had she been different, and differently placed, he would have blindly tried for anything he could get, in any possible way. But, as she was? ... He felt convinced he could never succeed in making her care for him; there was not the slightest chance of it. And, supposing even that he could? And here came in the delicacy and scruple of the man who had been married himself. He thought he wouldn't even wish to spoil, by the vulgarity of compromising, or by the shadow of a secret, the serenity of her face, the gay prettiness of that life. No, he wouldn't if he could. And yet how exciting it would be to rouse her from that cool composure. She was rather enigmatic. But he thought she could be roused. And she was so clever. How well she would carry it off! How she would never bore a man! And he suddenly imagined a day with her in the country. . . . Then he thought that his imagination was flying on far too fast. He decided not to be a hopeless fool, but just to go ahead, and talk to her, and get to know her; not to think too much about her. She needn't even know how he felt. To idolise her from a distance would be quite delightful enough. When a passion is not realised, he thought, it fades away, or becomes ideal worship—Dante— Petrarch—that sort of thing! It could never fade away in this case, he was sure. How pretty she was, how lovely her mouth was when she smiled! She had no prejudices, apparently; no affectations; how she played and sang that song again when he asked her! With what a delightful sense of humour she had dealt with him, and also with Bruce, at the Mitchells. Ottley must be a little difficult sometimes. She had read and thought; she had the same tastes as he. He wondered if she would have liked that thing in *The Academy*, on Gardens, that he had just read. He began looking for it. He thought he would send it to her, asking her opinion; then he would get an answer, and see her handwriting. You don't know a woman until you have had a letter from her.

But no—what a fool he would look! Besides he was going to see her to-night. It was about time to get ready.... Knowing subconsciously that he had made some slight favourable impression—at any rate that he hadn't repelled or bored her—he dressed with all the anxiety, joy and thrills of excitement of a boy of twenty; and no boy of twenty can ever feel these things as keenly or half as elaborately as a man nearly twice that age, since all the added experiences, disillusions, practice, knowledge and life of the additional years help to form a part of the same emotion, making it infinitely deeper, and all the stronger because so much more *averti* and conscious of itself.

He seemed so nervous while dressing that Soames, the valet, to whom he was a hero, ventured respectfully to hope there was nothing wrong.

"No. I'm all right," said Aylmer. "I'm never ill. I think Soames, I shall probably die of middle age."

He went out laughing, leaving the valet smiling coldly out of politeness.

Soames never understood any kind of jest. He took himself and everyone else seriously. But he already knew perfectly well that his master had fallen in love last night, and he disapproved very strongly. He thought all that sort of thing ought to be put a stop to.

CHAPTER VIII

ARCHIE'S ESSAY

"MRS. OTTLEY," said Miss Townsend, "do you mind looking at this essay of Archie's? I really don't know what to think of it. I think it shows talent, except the spelling. But it's *very* naughty of him to have written what is at the end."

Edith took the paper and read:

"Trays of Character

trays of character will always show threw how ever much you may polish it up trays of character will always show threw the grane of the wood.

A burd will keep on singing because he wants to and they can't help doing what it wants this is instinkt. and it is the same with trays of charicter. having thus shown my theory that trays of carocter will always show threw in spite of all trubble and in any circemstances whatever I will conclude Archibald Bruce Ottley please t.o."

On the other side of the paper was written very neatly, still in Archie's writing:

"3 LINDEN MANSIONS,
CADOGAN SQUARE,
KNIGHTSBRIDGE.

Second Floor

1. Mr. Bruce Ottley (F. O.)
2. Mrs. Bruce Ottley
3. Master Archibald Bruce Ottley
4. Little *beast*
5. Mary Johnson housemaid
6. Miss Thrupp Cook
7. Marie maid
8. Dorothy Margaret Miss Townsend governess
9. Ellen Maud Parrot nurse."

"Do you see?" said Miss Townsend. "It's his way of slyly calling poor Dilly a beast, because he's angry with her. Isn't it a shame? What shall I do?"

Both of them laughed and enjoyed it.

"Archie, what is the meaning of this? Why did you make this census of your home?" Edith asked him gently.

"Why, I didn't make senses of my home; I just wrote down who lived here."

Edith looked at him reproachfully.

"Well, I didn't call Dilly a beast. I haven't broken Miss Townsend's rules. She made a new rule I wasn't to call her a beast before breakfast——"

"What, you're allowed to call her these awful names after breakfast?"

"No. She made a rule before breakfast I wasn't to call Dilly a beast, and I haven't. How did you know it meant her anyway? It might have meant somebody else."

"That's prevaricating; it's mean—not like you, Archie."

"Well, I never called her a beast. No one can say I did. And besides, anybody would have called her a beast after how she went on."

"What are you angry with the child for?"

"Oh, she bothers so. The moment I imitate the man with the German accent she begins to cry. She says she doesn't like me to do it. She says she can't bear me to. Then she goes and tells Miss Townsend I slapped her, and Miss Townsend blames me."

"Then you shouldn't have slapped her; it was horrid of you; you ought to remember she's a little girl and weaker than you."

"I did remember . . ."

"Oh, Archie!"

"Well, I'll make it up if she begs my pardon;

not unless she does I sha'n't," said Archie magnanimously.

"I shall certainly not allow her to do anything of the kind."

At this moment Dilly came in, with her finger in her tiny mouth, and went up to Archie, drawling with a pout, and in a whining voice:

"I didn't *mean* to."

Archie beamed at once.

"That's all right, Dilly," he said forgivingly.

Then he turned to his mother.

"Mother, have you got that paper?"

"Yes, I have indeed!"

"Well, cross out—*that*, and put in Aspasia Matilda Ottley. Sorry, Dilly!" He kissed her, and they ran off together hand in hand; looking like cherubs, and laughing musically.

CHAPTER IX

AYLMER

AT the Carlton Aylmer had easily persuaded Bruce and Edith to dine with him next day, although they were engaged to the elder Mrs. Ottley already. He said he expected two or three friends, and he convinced them they must come too. It is only in London that people meet for the first time at a friend's house, and then, if they take to each other, practically live together for weeks after. No matter what social engagements they may happen to have, these are all thrown aside for the new friend. London people, with all their correctness, are really more unconventional than any other people in the world. For instance, in Paris such a thing could never happen in any kind of *monde*, unless, perhaps, it were among artists and Bohemians; and even then it would be their great object to prove to one another that they were not wanting in distractions and were very much in demand;

the lady, especially, would make the man wait for an opportunity of seeing her again, from calculation, to make herself seem of more value. Such second-rate solicitudes would never even occur to Edith. But she had a scruple about throwing over old Mrs. Ottley.

"Won't your mother be disappointed?" Edith asked.

"My dear Edith, you can safely leave that to me. Of course she'll be disappointed, but you can go round and see her, and speak to her nicely and tell her that after all we can't come because we've got another engagement."

"And am I to tell her it's a subsequent one? Otherwise she'll wonder we didn't mention it before."

"Don't be in a hurry, dear. Don't rush things; remember . . . she's my mother. Perhaps to you, Edith, it seems a rather old-fashioned idea, and I daresay you think it's rot, but to me there's something very sacred about the idea of a mother." He lit a cigarette and looked in the glass.

"Yes, dear. Then, don't you think we really ought to have kept our promise to dine with her? She'll probably be looking forward to it. I daresay she's asked one or two people she thinks we like, to meet us."

"Circumstances alter cases, Edith. If it comes to that, Aylmer Ross has got two or three people coming to dine with him whom he thinks we might like. He said so himself. That's why he's asked us."

"Yes, but he can't have asked them on purpose, Bruce, because, you see, we didn't know him on Thursday."

"Well, why should he have asked them on purpose? *How* you argue! *How* you go on! It really seems to me you're getting absurdly exacting and touchy, Edith dear. I believe all those flowers from the embassy have positively turned your head. *Why* should he have asked them on purpose? You admit yourself that we didn't even know the man last Thursday, and yet you expect——" Bruce stopped. He had got into a slight tangle.

Edith looked away. She had not quite mastered the art of the inward smile.

"Far better, in my opinion," continued Bruce, walking up and down the room.— "Now, don't interrupt me in your impulsive way, but hear me out—it would be far more kind and sensible in every way for you to sit right down at that little writing-table, take out your stylographic pen and write and tell my mother that I have a bad attack of influenza.... Yes; one should always be considerate to one's parents. I suppose it really is the way I was brought up that makes me feel this so keenly," he explained.

Edith sat down to the writing-table. "How bad is your influenza?"

"Oh, not very bad; because it would worry her: a slight attack.—Stop! Not so very slight— we must let her think it's the ordinary kind, and then she'll think it's catching and she won't come here for a few days, and that will avoid our going into the matter in detail, which would be better."

"If she thinks it's catching, dear, she'll want Archie and Dilly, and Miss Townsend and Nurse to go and stay with her in South Kensington, and that will be quite an affair."

"Right as usual; very thoughtful of you; you're a clever little woman sometimes, Edith. Wait!"—he put up his hand with a gesture frequent with him, like a policeman stopping the traffic at Hyde Park Corner. "Wait!— leave out the influenza altogether, and just say I've caught a slight chill."

"Yes. Then she'll come over at once, and you'll have to go to bed."

"My dear Edith," said Bruce, "you're over-anxious; I shall do nothing of the kind. There's no need that I should be laid up for this. It's not serious."

He was beginning to believe in his own illness, as usual.

"Air! (I want to go round to the club)—tonic treatment!—that's the thing!—that's often the very best thing for a chill—this sort of chill. . . . Ah, that will do very nicely. Very neatly written. . . . Good-bye, dear."

As soon as Bruce had gone out Edith rang up the elder Mrs. Ottley on the telephone, and relieved her anxiety in advance. They were great friends; the sense of humour possessed by her mother-in-law took the sting out of the relationship.

The dinner at Aylmer's house was a great success. Bruce enjoyed himself enormously, for he liked nothing better in the world than to give his opinion. And Aylmer was specially anxious for his view as to the authenticity of a little Old Master he had acquired, and took notes, also, of a word of advice with regard to electric lighting, admitting he was not a very practical man, and Bruce evidently was.

Edith was interested and pleased to go to the house of her new friend and to reconstruct the scene as it must have been when Mrs. Aylmer Ross had been there.

Freddy, the boy, was at school, but there

was a portrait of him. Evidently he resembled his father. The sketch represented him with the same broad forehead, smooth, dense light hair, pale blue eyes under eyebrows with a slight frown in them, and the charming mouth rather fully curved, expressing an amiable and pleasure-loving nature. The boy was good-looking, but not, Edith thought, as handsome as Aylmer.

The only other woman present was Lady Everard, a plump, talkative, middle-aged woman in black; the smiling widow of Lord Everard, and well known for her lavish musical hospitality and her vague and indiscriminate good nature. She bristled with aigrettes and sparkled with diamonds and determination. She was marvellously garrulous about nothing in particular. She was a woman who never stopped talking for a single moment, but in a way that resembled leaking rather then laying down the law. Tepidly, indifferently and rather amusingly she prattled on without ceasing, on every subject under the sun, and was socially a valuable help, because where she was there was never an awkward pause—or any other kind.

Vincy was there and young Cricker, whose occasional depressed silences were alternated with what he called a certain amount of sparkling chaff.

Lady Everard told Edith that she felt quite like a sort of mother to Aylmer.

"Don't you think it's sad, Mrs. Ottley," she said, when they were alone, "to think that the dear fellow has no wife to look after this dear little house? It always seems to me such a pity, but still, I always say, at any rate Aylmer's married once, and that's more than most of them do nowadays. It's simply horse's work to get them to do it at all. Sometimes I think it's perfectly disgraceful. And yet I can't help seeing how sensible it is of them too; you know, when you think of it, what with one thing and another, what does a man of the present day need a wife for? What with the flats, where everything on earth is done for them, and the kindness of friends—just think how bachelors are spoilt by their married friends!—and their clubs, and the frightful expense of everything, it seems to me, as a general rule, that the average man must be madly unselfish or a perfect idiot to marry at all—that's what it seems to me—don't you? When you think of all the responsibilities they take upon themselves!—and I'm sure there are not many modern wives who expect to do anything on earth but have their bills and bridge debts paid, and their perpetual young men asked to dinner, and one thing and another.

Of course, though, there are some exceptions."
She smiled amiably. "Aylmer tells me you have two children; very sweet of you, I'm sure. What darling pets they must be! Angels!—Angels! Oh, I'm so fond of children! But, particularly—isn't it funny?—when they're not there, because I can't stand their noise. Now my little grandchildren—my daughter Eva's been married ten years—Lady Lindley, you know—hers are perfect pets and heavenly angels, but I can't stand them for more than a few minutes at a time. I have nerves, so much so, do you know (partly because I go in a good deal for music and intellect and so on), so much so, that I very nearly had a rest cure at the end of last season, and I should have had, probably, but that new young French singer came over with a letter of introduction to me, and of course I couldn't desert him, but had to do my very best. Ever heard him sing? Yes, you would, of course. Oh, how wonderful it is!"

Edith waited in vain for a pause to say she didn't know the name of the singer. Lady Everard went on, leaning comfortably back in Aylmer's arm-chair.

"Willie Cricker dances very prettily, too; he came to one of my evenings and had quite a success. Only an amateur, of course; but rather nice. However, like all amateurs he wants to perform only when people would rather he didn't, and when they want him to he won't; he refuses. That's the amateur all over. The professional comes up to the scratch when wanted and stops when the performance is not required. It's all the difference in the world, isn't it, Mrs. Ottley? Still, he's a nice boy. Are you fond of music?"

"Very. Really fond of it; but I'm only a listener."

Lady Everard seemed delighted and brightened up.

"Oh, you don't sing or play?—you must come to one of my Musical Evenings. We have all the stars in the season at times—dear Melba and Caruso—and darling Bemberg and dear Debussy! Oh! don't laugh at my enthusiasm, my dear; but I'm quite music-mad—and then, of course, we have any amount of amateurs, and all the new young professionals that are coming on. In my opinion Paul La France, that's the young man I was telling you about, will be one of the very very best—quite at the top of the tree, and I'm determined he shall. But of course, he needs care and encouragement. I think of his giving a *Conférence*, in which he'll lecture on his own singing. I shall be on the platform to make a sort of introductory speech and Monti, of course, will accompany. He is the only accompanist that counts. But then I suppose he's been accompanying somebody or other ever since he was a little boy, so it's second nature to him. And you must come, and bring your husband. Does he go with you to places? Very nice of him. Nowadays if husbands and wives don't occasionally go to the same parties they have hardly any opportunity of meeting at all; that's what I always say. But then, of course, *you're* still almost on your honeymoon, aren't you? Charming!"

In the dining-room Cricker was confiding in Aylmer, while Vincy and Bruce discussed the Old Master.

"Awful, you know," Cricker said, in a low voice—"this girl's mania for me! I get wires and telephones all day long; she hardly gives me time to shave. And she's jolly pretty, so I don't like to chuck it; in fact, I daren't. But her one cry is 'Cold; cold; cold!' She says I'm as cold as a stone. What do you think of that?"

"You may be a stone, and a rolling one at that," said Aylmer, "but there are other pebbles on the beach, I daresay."

"I bet not one of them as stony as I am!" cried Cricker.

Cricker came a little nearer, lowering his voice again.

"It's a very peculiar case," he said proudly.

"Of course; it always is."

"You see, she's frightfully pretty, on the stage, *and* married! One of the most awkward positions a person can be in. Mind you, I'm sorry for her. I thought of consulting you about something if you'll give me a minute or two, old chap."

He took out a letter-case.

"I don't mean I'll show you this—oh no, I can't show it—it isn't compromising."

"Of course not. No one really likes to show a really lukewarm love letter. Besides, it would hardly be——"

Cricker put the case back.

"My dear chap! I wasn't going to show it to you—I shouldn't dream of such a thing—to anybody; but I was just going to read you out a sentence from which you can form an opinion of my predicament. It's no good mincing matters, old boy, the woman is crazy mad about me—there you've got it straight—in a nutshell.—Crazy!"

"She certainly can't be very sane," returned Aylmer.

Before the end of the evening Aylmer had arranged to take the Ottleys to see a play that was having a run. After this he dropped in to tea to discuss it and Bruce kept him to dinner.

Day after day went on, and they saw him continually. He had never shown by word or manner any more of his sentiment than on the second occasion when they had met, but Edith was growing thoroughly accustomed to this new interest, and it certainly gave a zest to her existence, for she knew, as women do know, or at any rate she believed, that she had an attraction for him, which he didn't intend to give away. The situation was pleasant and, notwithstanding Vincy's slight anxiety, she persisted in seeing nothing in it to fear in any way. Aylmer didn't even flirt.

One day, at Vincy's rooms, she thought he seemed different.

Vincy, with all his gentle manner, had in art an extraordinary taste for brutality and violence, and his rooms were covered with pictures by Futurists and Cubists, wild studies by wild men from Tahiti and a curious collection of savage ornaments and weapons.

"I don't quite see Vincy handling that double-eged Chinese sword, do you?" said Aylmer, laughing.

"No, nor do I; but I do like to look at it," Vincy said.

They went into the little dining-room, which was curiously furnished with a green marble dining-table, narrow, as in the pictures of the

Last Supper, at which the guests could sit on one side only, to be waited on from the other. On it as decoration (it was laid for two, side by side) were some curious straw mats, a few laurel leaves, a little marble statuette of Pan, and three Tangerine oranges.

"Oh, Vincy, do tell me—what are you going to eat to-night?" Edith exclaimed. "Unless you're with other people I can never imagine you sitting down to a proper meal."

"Eat? Oh, a nice orange, I think," said he. "Sometimes when I'm alone I just have a nice egg and a glass of water. I do myself very well. Don't worry about me, Edith."

When they were alone for a moment Aylmer looked out of the window. It was rather high up, and they looked down on the hustling crowds of people pushing along through the warm air in Victoria Street.

"It's getting decent weather," he said.

"Yes, quite warm."

They always suddenly talked commonplaces when they were first left alone.

"I may be going away pretty soon," he said.

"Going away! Oh, where?"

"I'm not quite sure yet."

There was a pause.

"Well, you'll come to tea to-morrow, won't you?" said Edith.

"Yes, indeed, thank you—thank you so much. I shall look forward to it. At five?" He spoke formally.

"At four," said Edith.

"I shall be lunching not very far from you to-morrow."

"At a quarter to four," said Edith.

"I wonder who this other place is laid for," said Aylmer, looking at the table.

"How indiscreet of you! So do I. One must find out."

"How? By asking?"

"Good heavens, no!" cried Edith. "What an extraordinary idea!"

CHAPTER X

SHOPPING CHEZ SOI

EDITH was expecting Aylmer to call that afternoon before he went away. She was surprised to find how perturbed she was at the idea of his going away. He had become almost a part of their daily existence, and seeing him was certainly quite the most amusing and exciting experience she had ever had. And now it was coming to an end. Some obscure clairvoyance told her that his leaving and telling her of it in this vague way had some reference to her; but perhaps (she thought) she was wrong; perhaps it was simply that, after the pleasant intercourse and semi-intimacy of the last few weeks, he was going to something that interested him more? He was a widower; and still a young man. Perhaps he was in love with someone. This idea was far from agreeable, although except the first and second time they met he had never said a word that could be described even as flirtation. He showed admiration for her, and pleasure in her society, but he rarely saw her alone. The few visits and *tête-à-têtes* had always begun by conventional commonplace phrases and embarrassment, and had ended in a delightful sympathy, in animated conversation, in a flowing confidence and gaiety, and in long discussions on books, and art, and principally people. That was all. In fact he had become, in two or three weeks, in a sense *l'ami de la maison*; they went everywhere with him and met nearly every day, and Bruce appeared to adore him. It was entirely different from her long and really intimate friendship with Vincy. Vincy was her confidant, her friend. She could tell *him* everything, and she did, and he confided in her and told her all except one side of his life, of which she was aware, but to which she never referred. This was his secret romance with a certain girl artist of whom he never spoke, although Edith knew that some day he would tell her about that also.

But with Aylmer there was, and would always be, less real freedom and impersonal frankness, because there was so much more self-consciousness; in fact because there was an unacknowledged but very strong mutual physical attraction. Edith had, however, felt until now merely the agreeable excitement of knowing that a man she liked, and in whom she was immensely interested, was growing apparently devoted to her, while *she* had always believed that she would know how to deal with the case in such a way that it could never lead to anything more—that is to say, to more than *she* wished.

And now, he was going away. Why? And where? However, the first thing to consider was that she would see him to-day. The result of this consideration was the obvious one. She must do some shopping.

Edith was remarkably feminine in every attribute, in manner, in movement and in appearance; indeed, for a woman of the present day unusually and refreshingly feminine. Yet she had certain mental characteristics which were entirely unlike most women. One was her extreme aversion for shops, and indeed for going into any concrete little details. It has been said that her feeling for dress was sure and unerring. But it was entirely that of the artist; it was impressionistic. Edith was very clever, indeed, most ingenious, in managing practical affairs, as long as she was the director, the general of the campaign. But she did not like carrying out in detail her plans. She liked to be the architect, not the workman.

For example, the small household affairs in

the flat went on wheels; everything was almost always perfect. But Edith did not rattle her housekeeping keys, or count the coals, nor did she even go through accounts, or into the kitchen every day. The secret was simple. She had a good cook and housekeeper, who managed all these important but tedious details admirably, under her suggestions. In order to do this Edith had to practise a little fraud on Bruce, a justifiable and quite unselfish one. She gave the cook and housekeeper a quarter of her dress allowance, in addition to the wages Bruce considered sufficient; because Bruce believed that they could not afford more than a certain amount for a cook, while he admitted that Edith, who had a few hundred pounds a year of her own, might need to spend this on dress. Very little of it went on dress, although Edith was not very economical. But she had a plan of her own; she knew that to be dressed in a very ordinary style (that is to say, simple, conventional, *comme il faut*) suited her, by throwing her unusual beauty into relief. Occasionally a touch of individuality was added, when she wanted to have a special effect. But she never entered a shop; very rarely interviewed a milliner. It was always done for her. She was easy to dress, being tall, slim and remarkably pretty. She thought that most women make a great mistake in allowing dress to be the master instead of the servant of their good looks; many women were, she considered, entirely crushed and made insignificant by the beauty of their clothes. The important thing was to have a distinguished appearance, and this cannot, of course, easily be obtained without expensive elegance. But Edith was twenty-eight, and looked younger, so she could dress simply.

This morning Edith had telephoned to her friend, Miss Bennett, an old schoolfellow who had nothing to do, and adored commissions. Edith, sitting by the fire or at the 'phone, gave her orders, which were always decisive, short and yet meticulous. Miss Bennett was a little late this morning, and Edith had been getting quite anxious to see her. When she at last arrived—she was a nondescript-looking girl, with a small hat squashed on her head, a serge coat and skirt, black gloves and shoes with spats—Edith greeted her rather reproachfully with:

"You're late, Grace."

"Sorry," said Grace.

The name suited her singularly badly. She was plain, but had a pleasant face, a pink complexion, small bright eyes, protruding teeth and a scenario for a figure, merely a collection of bones on which a dress could be hung. She was devoted to Edith, and to a few other friends of both sexes, of whom she made idols. She was hard, abrupt, enthusiastic, ignorant and humorous.

"Sorry, but I had to do a lot of——"

"All right," interrupted Edith. "You couldn't help it. Listen to what I want you to do."

"Go ahead," said Miss Bennett, taking out a note-book and pencil.

Edith spoke in her low, soft, impressive voice, rather slowly.

"Go anywhere you like and bring me back two or three perfectly simple tea-gowns—you know the sort of shape, rather like evening cloaks—straight lines—none of the new draperies and curves—in red, blue and black."

"On appro.?" asked Miss Bennett.

"On anything you like, but made of Liberty satin, with a dull surface."

"There's no such thing." Grace Benett laughed. "You mean charmeuse, or crepe-de-chine, perhaps?"

"Call it what you like, only get it. You must bring them back in a taxi."

"Extravagant girl!"

"They're not to cost more than—oh! not much," added Edith, "at the most."

"Economical woman! Why not have a really good tea-gown while you're about it?"

"These *will* be good. I want to have a hard outl ne like a Fergusson."

"Oh, really? What's that?"

"Never mind. And suppose you can't get the shape, Grace."

"Yes?"

"Bring some evening cloaks—the kimonoish kind—I could wear one over a lace blouse; it would look exactly the same."

"Edith, what curious ideas you have! But you're right enough. Anything else?" said Miss Bennett, standing up, ready to go. "I like shopping for you. You know what you want."

"Buy me an azalea, not a large one, and a bit of some dull material of the same colour to drape round it."

"How extraordinary it is the way you hate anything shiny!" exclaimed Miss Bennett, making a note.

"I know; I only like *mat* effects. Oh, and in case I choose a light-coloured gown, get me just one very large black velvet orchid, too."

"Right. That all?"

Edith looked at her shoes; they were perfect, tiny, pointed and made of black suède. She decided they would do.

"Yes, that's all, dear."

"And might I kindly ask," said Miss Bennett, getting up, "any particular reason for all this? Are you going to have the flu, or a party, or what?"

"No," said Edith, who was always frank when it was possible. "I'm expecting a visitor who's never seen me in anything but a coat and skirt, or in evening dress."

"Oh! He wants a change, does he?"

"Don't be vulgar, Grace. Thanks awfully, dear. You're really kind."

They both laughed, and Edith gently pushed her friend out of the room. Then she sat down on a sofa, put up her feet, and began to read *Rhythm* to divert her thoughts. Vincy had brought it to convert her to Post-Impressionism.

When Archie and Dilly were out, and Edith, who always got up rather early, was alone, she often passed her morning hours in reading, dreaming, playing the piano, or even in thinking. She was one of the few women who really can think, and enjoy it. This morning she soon put down the mad clever little prophetic Oxford journal. Considering she was usually the most reposeful woman in London, she was rather restless to-day. She glanced round the little room; there was nothing in it to distract or irritate, or even to suggest a train of thought;

except perhaps the books; everything was calming and soothing, with a touch of gaiety in the lightness of the wall decorations. An azalea, certainly, would be a good note. The carpet, and almost everything in the room, was green, except the small white enamelled piano. To-day she felt that she wanted to use all her influence to get Aylmer to confide in her more. Perhaps he was slipping away from her—she would have been only a little incident in his existence—while *she* certainly wished it to go on. Seeing this, perhaps it oughtn't to go on. She wondered if he would laugh or be serious to-day ... whether ...

*

Miss Bennett had come up in the lift with a heap of cardboard boxes, and the azalea. A taxi was waiting at the door.

Edith opened the boxes, cutting the string with scissors. She put four gowns out on the sofa. Grace explained that two were cloaks, two were gowns—all she could get.

"That's the one," said Edith, taking out one of a deep blue colour, like an Italian sky on a coloured picture post-card. It had a collar of the same deep blue, spotted with white—a birdseye effect. Taking off her coat Edith slipped the gown over her dress, and went to her room (followed closely by Miss Bennett) to see herself in the long mirror.

"Perfect!" said Edith. "Only I must cut off those buttons. I hate buttons."

"How are you going to fasten it, then, dear?"

"With hooks and eyes. Marie can sew them on."

The deep blue with the white spots had a vivid and charming effect, and suited her blonde colouring; she saw she was very pretty in it, and was pleased.

"Aren't you going to try the others on, dear?" asked Grace.

"No; what's the good? This one will do."

"Right. Then I'll take them back."

"You're sweet. Won't you come back to lunch?"

"I'll come back to lunch to-morrow," said Miss Bennett, "and you can tell me about your tea-party. Oh, and here's a little bit of stuff for the plant. I suppose you'll put the azalea into the large pewter vase?"

"Yes, and I'll tie this round its neck."

"Sorry it's cotton," said Miss Bennett. "I couldn't get any silk the right colour."

"Oh, I like cotton, if only it's not called sateen! Good-bye, darling. You're delightfully quick!"

"Yes, I don't waste time," said Miss Bennett. "Mother says, too, that I'm the best shopper in the world." She turned round to add, "I'm dying to know why you want to look so pretty. Who is it?"

With a quiet smile, Edith dismissed her.

CHAPTER XI

P.P.C.

"IT always seems to me so unlike you," Aylmer said (he had arrived punctually at twenty minutes to four)—"your extreme fondness for newspapers. You're quite celebrated as a collector of Last Editions, aren't you?"

"I know it's very unliterary of me, but I enjoy reading newspapers better than reading anything else in the world. After all, it's contemporary history, that's my defence. But I suppose it is because I'm so intensely interested in life."

"Tell me exactly, what papers do you really read?"

She laughed. "Four morning papers—never mind their names—four evening papers; five Sunday papers: *The Academy*, *The Saturday Review*, *The Bookman*, *The World*, *The English Review*."

"Well, I think it's wicked of you to encourage

all this frivolity. And what price *The Queen*, *Home Notes*, or *The Tatler*?"

"Oh, we have those too—for Bruce."

"And does Archie show any of this morbid desire for journalism?"

"Oh yes. He takes in *Chums* and *Little Folks*."

"And I see you're reading *Rhythm*. That's Vincy's fault, of course."

"Perhaps it is."

"How do you find time for all this culture?"

"I read quickly, and what I have to do I do rather quickly."

"Is that why you never seem in a hurry? I think you're the only leisured-looking woman I know in London."

"I do think I've solved the problem of labour-saving; I've reduced it to a science."

"How?"

"By not working, I suppose."

"You're wonderful. And that blue...."

"Do you really think so?"

He was beginning to get carried away. He stood up and looked out of the window. The pink and white hyacinths were strongly scented in the warm air. He turned round.

She said demurely: "It will be nice weather for you to go away now, won't it?"

"I don't think so." He spoke impulsively. "I shall hate it; I shall be miserable."

"Really!" in a tone of great surprise.

"You're dying to ask me something," he said.

"Which am I dying to ask you: *where* you're going, or *why* you're going?" She gave her most vivid smile. He sat down with a sigh. People still sigh, sometimes, even nowadays.

"I don't know where I'm going; but I'll tell you why. . . . I'm seeing too much of you."

She was silent.

"You see, Mrs. Ottley, seeing a great deal of you is very entrancing, but it's dangerous."

"In what way?"

"Well—your society—you see one gets to feel one can't do without it, do you see?"

"But why should you do without it?"

He looked at her. "You mean there's no reason why we shouldn't keep on going to plays with Bruce, dining with Bruce, being always with Bruce?" (Bruce and Aylmer had become so intimate that they called each other by their Christian names.) "Don't you see, it makes one sometimes feel one wants more and more of you—of your society I mean. One could talk better alone."

"But you can come and see me sometimes, can't you?"

"Yes; that's the worst of all," he answered, with emphasis.

"Oh."

Aylmer spoke decidedly: "I'm not a man who could ever be a tame cat. And also I'm not, I hope, a man who—who would dare to think, or even wish, to spoil—to——"

"And is that really why you're going?" she asked gently.

"You're forcing me to answer you."

"And shall you soon forget all about it?"

He changed his position and sat next to her on the sofa.

"And so you won't miss me a bit," he said caressingly. "You wouldn't care if you never saw me again, would you?"

"Yes, I should care. Why, you know we're awfully good friends; I like you immensely."

"As much as Vincy?"

"Oh! So differently."

"I'm glad of that, at any rate!"

There was an embarrassed pause.

"So this is really the last time I'm to see you for ages, Mrs. Ottley?"

"But aren't we all going to the theatre tomorrow? With you, I mean? Bruce said so."

"Oh yes. I mean the last time alone. Yes, I've got a box for *The Moonshine Girl*. Bruce said you'd come. Lady Everard and Vincy will be there."

"That will be fun—I love that sort of show.

It takes one right away from life instead of struggling to imitate it badly like most plays."

"It's always delightful to hear what you say. And anything I see with *you* I enjoy, and believe to be better than it is," said Aylmer. "You know you cast a glamour over anything. But the next day I'm going away for three months at least."

"A long time."

"Is it? Will it seem long to you?"

"Why, of course. We shall—I shall miss you very much. I told you so."

"Really?" he insisted.

"Really," she smiled.

They looked at each other.

Edith felt less mistress of the situation than she had expected. She was faced with a choice; she felt it; she knew it. She didn't want him to go. Still, perhaps ... There was a vibration in the air. Suddenly a sharp ring was heard.

Overpowered by a sudden impulse, Aylmer seized her impetuously by the shoulders, kissed her roughly and at random before she could stop him, and said incoherently: "Edith! Good-bye. I love you, Edith," and then stood up by the mantelpiece.

"Mr. Vincy," announced the servant.

CHAPTER XII

"THE MOONSHINE GIRL"

THE next evening Bruce and Edith were going to the Society Theatre with Aylmer. It was their last meeting before he was to go away. Edith half expected that he would put it off, but there was no change made in the plans, and they met in the box as arranged.

Aylmer had expected during the whole day to hear that she had managed to postpone the party. At one moment he was frightened and rather horrified when he thought of what he had done. At another he was delighted and enchanted about it, and told himself that it was absolutely justified. After all, he couldn't do more than go away if he found he was too fond of her. No hero of romance could be expected to do more than that, and he wasn't a hero of romance; he didn't pretend to be. But he *was* a good fellow—and though Bruce's absurdities irritated him a great deal he had a feeling of delicacy towards him, and a scrupulousness that is not to be found every day. At other moments Aylmer swore to himself, cursing his impulsiveness, fearing she now would really not ever think of him as he wished, but as a hustling sort of brute. But no—he didn't care. He had come at last to close quarters with her. He had kissed the pretty little mouth that he had so often watched with longing. He admitted to himself that he had really wished to pose a little in her eyes: to be the noble hero in the third act who goes away from temptation. But who does not wish for the *beau rôle* before one's idol?

*

This meeting at the play to-night was the sort of anti-climax that is almost invariable in a London romance. How he looked forward to it! For after Vincy came in only a few banalities had been said. He was to see her now for the last time—the first time since he had given himself away to her. Probably it was only her usual kindness to others that prevented her getting out of the evening plans, he thought. Or—did she want to see him once more?

At dinner before the play Edith was very bright, and particularly pretty. Bruce, too, was in good spirits.

"It's rather sickening," he remarked, "Aylmer going away like this; we shall miss him horribly, sha'n't we? And then, where's the sense, Edith, in a chap leaving London where he's been the whole of the awful winter, just as it begins to be pleasant here? Pass the salt; don't spill it—that's unlucky. Not that I believe in any superstitious rot. I can see the charm of the quaint old ideas about black cats and so forth, but I don't for one moment attach any importance to them, nor to the number thirteen, nor any of that sort of bosh. Indeed as a matter of fact, I walked round a ladder only to-day rather than go under it. But that's simply because I don't go in for trying to be especially original."

"No, dear. I think you're quite right."

"And oddly enough—as I was trying to tell you just now, only you didn't seem to be listening—a black cat ran across my path only this afternoon." He smiled, gratified at the recollection.

"How do you mean, your path? I didn't know you had one—or that there were any paths about here."

"How literal women are! I mean *I* nearly ran over it in a taxi. When I say I nearly ran over it, I mean that a black cat on the same side of the taxi (if you must have details) ran away as the taxi drove on. ... Yes, Aylmer is a thoroughly good chap, and he and I have enormous sympathy. I don't know any man in the world with whom I have more intellectual sympathy than Aylmer Ross. Do you remember how I pointed him out to you at once at the Mitchells'? And sometimes when I think how you used to sneer at the Mitchells—oh, you did, you know, dear, before you knew them—and I remember all the trouble I had to get you to go there, I wonder—I simply wonder! Don't you see, through going there, as I advised, we've made one of the nicest friends we ever had."

"Really, Bruce, you didn't have *any* trouble to get me to go to the Mitchell's; you're forgetting. The trouble was I couldn't go there very well until I was asked. The very first time we were asked (if you recollect), we flew!"

"Flew? Why, we went on the wrong night. That doesn't look as if I was very keen about it! However, I'm not blaming you, dear. It wasn't your fault. Mind you," continued Bruce, "I consider the Society Theatre pure frivolity. But one thing I'll say, a bad show there is better than a good show anywhere else. There's always jolly music, pretty dresses, pretty girls—you don't mind my saying so, dear, do you?"

"No, indeed. I think so myself."

"Of course the first row of the chorus is not what it was when I was a bachelor," continued Bruce, frowning thoughtfully. "Either they're not so good-looking, or I don't admire them so much, or they don't admire *me* as much, or they're a different class, or—or—something!" he laughed.

"You're pleased to be facetious," remarked Edith.

"My dear girl, you know perfectly well I think there's no one else in the world like you. Wherever I go I always say there's no one to touch my wife. No one!"

Edith got up. "Very sweet of you."

"But," continued Bruce, "because I think you pretty, it doesn't follow that I think everybody else is hideous. I tell you that straight from the shoulder, and I must say this for you, dear, I've never seen any sign of jealousy on your part."

"I'd show it soon enough if I felt it—if I thought I'd any cause," said Edith; "but I didn't think I had."

Bruce gave a rather fatuous smile. "Oh, go and get ready, my dear," he answered. "Don't let's talk nonsense. Who's going to be there to-night, do you know?"

"Oh, only Lady Everard and Vincy."

"Lady Everard is a nice woman. You're going to that musical thing of hers, I suppose?"

"Yes, I suppose so."

"It's in the afternoon, and it's not very easy for me to get away in the afternoon, but to please you, I'll take you—see? I loathe music (except musical comedies), and I think if ever there was a set of appalling rotters—I feel inclined to knock them off the music-stool the way they go on at Lady Everard's—at the same time, some of them are very cultured and intelligent chaps, and *she's* a very charming woman. One can't get in a word edgeways, but *when* one does—well, she listens, and laughs at one's jokes, and that sort of thing. I think I'm rather glad you're not musical, Edith, it takes a woman away from her husband."

"Not musical! Oh dear! I thought I was," said Edith.

"Oh, anyhow, not when I'm there, so it doesn't matter. Besides, your being appreciative and that sort of thing is very nice. Look what a social success you've had at the Everards', for instance, through listening and understanding these things; it is not an accomplishment to throw away. No, Edith dear, I should tell you, if you would only listen to me, to keep up your music, but you won't; and there's an end of it. . . . That *soufflé* was really very good. Cook's improving. For a plain little cook like that, with such small wages, and no kitchenmaid, she does quite well."

"Oh yes, she's not bad," said Edith. She knew that if Bruce had been aware the cook's remuneration was adequate he would not have enjoyed his dinner.

*

They were in the box in the pretty theatre. Lady Everard, very smart in black, sparkling with diamonds, was already there with Aylmer. Vincy had not arrived.

The house was crammed to the ceiling. Gay, electrical music of exhilarating futility was being played by the orchestra. The scene consisted of model cottages; a chorus of pretty girls in striped cotton were singing. The heroine came on; she was well known for her smile, which had become public property on picture postcards and the Obosh bottles. She was dressed as a work-girl also, but in striped silk with a real lace apron and a few diamonds. Then the hero arrived. He wore a red shirt, brown boots, and had a tenor voice. He explained an interesting little bit of the plot, which included an eccentric will and other novelties. The humorous dandy of the play was greeted with shouts of joy by the chorus and equal enthusiasm by the audience. He agreed to change places with the hero, who wished to give up one hundred and forty thousand pounds a year to marry the heroine.

"Very disinterested," murmured Lady Everard. "Very nice of him, I'm sure. It isn't many people that would do a thing like that. A nice voice, too. Of course, this is not what *I* call good music, but it's very bright in its way, and the words—I always think these words are so clever. So witty. Listen to them—do listen to them, dear Mrs. Ottley."

They listened to the beautiful words sung, of which the refrain ran as follows:—

"*The Author told the Actor,*
(The Actor had a fit).
The Box Office man told the Programme-girl,
The Theatre all was in quite a whirl.
The call-boy told the Chorus.
(Whatever could it be?)
The super asked the Manager,
What did the Censor see?"

"Charming," murmured Lady Everard; "brilliant—I know his father so well."

"Whose father—the censor's?"

"Oh, the father of the composer—a very charming man. When he was young he used to come to my parties—my Wednesdays. I used to have Wednesdays then. I don't have Wednesdays now. I think it better to telephone at the last minute any particular day for my afternoons because, after all, you never

"THE MOONSHINE GIRL" 119

know when the artists one wants are disengaged, does one? You're coming on Wednesday to hear Paul La France sing, dear Mrs. Ottley?"

Edith smiled and nodded assent, trying to stop the incessant trickle of Lady Everard's leaking conversation. She loved theatres, and she enjoyed hearing every word, which was impossible while there was more dialogue in the box than on the stage; also, Aylmer was sitting behind her.

The comic lady now came on; there were shrieks of laughter at her unnecessary and irrelevant green boots and crinoline, and Cockney accent. She proposed to marry the hero, who ran away from her. There was more chorus; and the curtain fell.

In the interval Vincy arrived. He and Bruce went into the little salon behind the box. Lady Everard joined them there. Edith and Aylmer looked round the house. The audience at the Society Theatre is a special one; as at the plays in which the favourite actor-managers and *jeunes premiers* perform there are always far more women than men, at this theatre there are always far more men than women.

The stage box opposite our friends was filled with a party of about ten men.

"It looks like a jury," said Edith. "Perhaps it is."

"Probably a board of directors," said Aylmer.

The first two rows of the stalls were principally occupied by middle-aged and rather elderly gentlemen. Many had grey moustaches and a military bearing. Others were inclined to be stout; with brilliant, exuberant manners and very dark hair that simply wouldn't lie flat. There were a great many parties made up like those of our friends—of somebody in love with somebody, surrounded by chaperons. These were the social people, and also there were a certain number of young men with pretty women who were too fashionably dressed, too much made up, and who were looking forward too much to supper. These ladies seemed inclined to crab the play, and to find unimportant little faults with the unimportant little actresses. There were many Americans—who took it seriously; and altogether one could see it was an immense success; in other words everyone had paid for their seats....

*

The play was over; Aylmer had not had a word with Edith. He was going away the next day, and he asked them all to supper. Of course he drove Edith, and Lady Everard took the other two in her motor....

"You're an angel if you've forgiven me," he said, as they went out.

CHAPTER XIII

THE SUPPER-PARTY

"HAVE you forgiven me?" he asked anxiously, as soon as they were in the dark shelter of the cab.

"Yes, oh yes. Please don't let's talk about it any more. . . . What time do you start to-morrow?"

"You think I ought to go then?"

"You say so."

"But you'd rather I remained here; rather we should go on as we are—wouldn't you?"

"Well, you know *I* should never have dreamt of suggesting you should go away. I like you to be here."

"At any cost to me? No, Edith; I can't stand it. And since I've told you it's harder. Your knowing makes it harder."

"I should have thought that if you liked anyone so *very* much, you would want to see them all the time, as much as possible, always —even with other people . . . anything rather than not see them—be away altogether. At least, that's how I should feel."

"No doubt you would; that's a woman's view. And besides, you see, you don't care!"

"The more I cared, the less I should go away, I think."

"But, haven't I tried? And I can't bear it. You don't know how cruel you are with your sweetness, Edith. . . . Oh, put yourself in my place! How do you suppose I feel when I've been with you like this, near you, looking at you, delighting in you the whole evening—and then, after supper, you go away with Bruce? *You've* had a very pleasant evening, no doubt; it's all right for you to feel you've got me, as you know you have—and with no fear, no danger. Yes, *you* enjoy it!"

"Oh, Aylmer!"

He saw in the half-darkness that her eyes looked reproachful.

"I didn't mean it. I'm sorry—I'm always being sorry." His bitter tone changed to gentleness. "I want to speak to you now, Edith. We haven't much time. Don't take away your hand a minute. . . . I always told you, didn't I, that the atmosphere round you is so clear that I feel with you I'm in the Palace of Truth? You're so *real*. You're the only woman I ever met who really cared for truth. You're not afraid of it; and you're as straight and honourable as a man! I don't mean you can't diplomatise if you choose, of course, and better than anyone; but it isn't your nature to deceive yourself, nor anyone else. I recognise that in you. I love it. And that's why I can't pretend or act with you; I must be frank."

"Please, do be frank."

"I love you. I'm madly in love with you. I adore you."

Aylmer stopped, deeply moved at the sound of his own words. Few people realise the effect such words have on the speaker. Saying them to her was a great joy, and an indulgence, but it increased painfully his passionate feeling, making it more accentuated and acute. To let himself go verbally was a wild, bitter pleasure. It hurt him, and he enjoyed it.

"And I'd do anything in the world to get you. And I'd do anything in the world for you, too. And if you cared for me I'd go away all the same. At least, I believe I should. . . . We shall be there in a minute.

"Listen, dear. I want you, occasionally, to write to me; there's no earthly reason why you shouldn't. I'll let you know my address. It will prevent my being too miserable, or rushing back. And will you do something else for me?"

"Anything."

"Angel! Well, when you write, call me Aylmer. You never have yet, in a letter. Treat me just like a friend—as you treat Vincy. Tell me what you're doing, where you're going, who you see; about Archie and Dilly; about your new dresses and hats; what you're reading—any little thing, so that I'm still in touch with you."

"Yes, I will; I shall like to. And don't be depressed, Aylmer. Do enjoy your journey; write to me, too."

"Yes, I'm going to write to you, but only in an official way, only for Bruce. And, listen. Take care of yourself. You're too unselfish. Do what *you* want sometimes, not what other people want all the time. Don't read too much by electric light and try your eyes. And don't go out in these thin shoes in damp weather—promise!"

She laughed a little—touched.

"Be a great deal with the children. I like to think of you with them. And I hope you won't be always going out," he continued, in a tone of unconscious command, which she enjoyed.... "Please don't be continually at Lady Everard's, or at the Mitchells', or anywhere. I hate you to be admired—how I hate it!"

"Fancy! And I was always brought up to

believe people are proud of what's called the 'success' of the people that they—like."

"Don't you believe it, Edith! That's all bosh—vanity and nonsense. At any rate, I know I'm not. In fact, as I can't have you myself, I would really like you to be shut up. Very happy, very well, with everything in the world you like, even thinking of me a little, but absolutely shut up! And if you did go out, for a breath of air, I should like no one to see you. I'd like you to cover up your head—wear a thick veil—and a thick loose dress!"

"You're very Oriental!" she laughed.

"I'm not a bit Oriental; I'm human. It's selfish, I suppose, you think? Well, let me tell you, if you care to know, that it's *love*, and nothing else, Edith. . . . Now, is there anything in the world I can do for you while I'm away? It would be kind to ask me. Remember I sha'n't see you for three months. I may come back in September. Can't I send you something —do *something* that you'd like? I count on you to ask me at any time if there's anything in the world I could do for you, no matter what!"

No woman could help being really pleased at such whole-hearted devotion and such Bluebeard-like views—especially when they were not going to be carried out. Edith was thrilled by the passionate emotion she felt near her.

How cold it would be when he had gone! He *was* nice, handsome, clever—a darling!

"Don't forget me, Aylmer. I don't want you to forget me. Later on we'll have a real friendship."

"*Friendship!* Don't use that word. It's so false—such humbug—for *me* at any rate. To say I could care for you as a friend is simply blasphemy! How can it be possible for *me*? But I'll try. Thanks for *any*thing! You're an angel—I'll try."

"And it's horribly inconsistent, and no doubt very wicked of me, but, do you know, I should be rather pained if I heard you had fallen in love with someone else."

"Ah, that would be impossible!" he cried. "Never—never! It's the real thing; there never was anyone like you, there never will be. Let me look at you once more.... Oh, Edith! And now—here we are."

Edith took away her hand.

"Your scarf's coming off, you'll catch cold," said Aylmer, and as he was trying, rather awkwardly, to put the piece of blue chiffon round her head he drew the dear head to him and kissed her harshly. She could not protest; it was too final; besides, they were arriving; the cab stopped. Vincy came to the door.

"Welcome to Normanhurst!" cried Vincy,

THE SUPPER-PARTY 127

with unnecessary facetiousness, giving them a slightly anxious glance. He thought Edith had more colour than usual. Aylmer was pale.

The supper was an absolute and complete failure; the guests displayed the forced gaiety and real depression, and constrained absent-mindedness, of genuine and hopeless boredom. Except for Lady Everard's ceaseless flow of empty prattle the pauses would have been too obvious. Edith, for whom it was a dreary anti-climax, was rather silent. Aylmer talked more, and a little more loudly, than usual, and looked worn. Bruce, whom champagne quickly saddened, became vaguely reminiscent and communicative about old, dead, forgotten grievances of the past, while Vincy, who was a little shocked at what he saw (and he always saw everything), did his very best, just saving the entertainment from being a too disastrous frost.

"Well! Good luck!" said Aylmer, lifting his glass with sham conviviality. "I start to-morrow morning by the Orient Express."

"Hooray!" whispered Vincy primly.

"Doesn't it sound romantic and exciting?" Edith said. "The two words together are so delightfully adventurous. Orient—the languid East, and yet express—quickness, speed. It's a fascinating blend of ideas."

"Whether it's adventurous or not isn't the question, my dear girl; I only wish we were going too," said Bruce, with a sigh; "but, I never can get away from my wretched work, to have any fun, like you lucky chaps, with no responsibilities or troubles! I suppose perhaps we may take the children to Westgate for Whitsuntide, and that's about all. Not that there isn't quite a good hotel there, and of course it's all right for me, because I shall play golf all day and run up to town when I want to. Still, it's very different from one of these jolly long journeys that you gay bachelors can indulge in."

"But I'm not a gay bachelor. My boy is coming to join me in the summer holidays, wherever I am," said Aylmer.

"Ah, but that's not the point. I should like to go with you now—at once. Don't you wish we were both going, Edith? Why aren't we going with him to-morrow?"

"Surely June's just the nice time in London, Bruce," said Vincy, in his demure voice.

"Won't it be terribly hot?" said Lady Everard vaguely. She always thought every place must be terribly hot. "Venice? Are you going to Venice? Delightful! The Viennese are so charming, and the Austrian officers—— Oh, you're going to Sicily first? Far too hot. Paul

La France—the young singer, you know—told me that when he was in Sicily his voice completely altered; the heat quite affected the *velouté* of his voice, as the French call it—and what a voice it is at its best! It's not the *highest* tenor, of course, but the medium is so wonderfully soft and well developed. I don't say for a moment that he will ever be a Caruso, but as far as he goes—and he goes pretty far, mind— it's really wonderful. You're coming on Wednesday, aren't you, dear Mrs. Ottley? Ah!" ... She stopped and held up her small beaded fan, "what's that the band's playing? I know it so well; everyone knows it; it's either *Pagliacci* or *Bohème*, or *some*thing. No, isn't it really? What is it? All the old Italian operas are coming in again, by the way, you know, my dear ... *Rigoletto*, *Lucia*, *Traviata*—the *bel canto*—that sort of thing; there's nothing like it for showing off the voice. Wagner's practically gone out (at least what *I* call out), and I always said Debussy wouldn't last. Paul La France still clings to Brahms—Brahms suits his voice better than anyone else. He always falls back on Brahms, and dear de Lara; and Tosti; of course, Tosti. I remember ..."

Aylmer and his guests had reached the stage of being apparently all lost in their own thoughts, and the conversation had been practically reduced to a disjointed monologue on music by Lady Everard, when the lights began to be lowered, and the party broke up.

"I'm coming to see you *so* soon," said Vincy.

CHAPTER XIV

THE LETTER

IT was about a fortnight later.
Edith and Bruce, from different directions, arrived at the same moment at their door, and went up together in the lift. On the little hall-table was a letter addressed to Edith. She took it up rather quickly, and went into the drawing-room. Bruce followed her.

"That a letter, Edith?"

"What do you suppose it is, Bruce?"

"What *could* I have supposed it was, Edith? A plum pudding?" He laughed very much.

"You are very humorous to-day, Bruce."

She sat down with her hat, veil and gloves on, holding the letter. She did not go to her room, because that would leave her no further retreat. Bruce sat down exactly opposite to her, with his coat and gloves on. He slowly drew off one glove, folded it carefully, and put it down. Then he said amiably, a little huskily:

"Letter from a friend?"

"I beg your pardon? What did you say, dear?"

He raised his voice unnecessarily:

"I said A LETTER FROM A FRIEND!"

She started. "Oh yes! I heard this time."

"Edith, I know of an excellent aurist in Bond Street. I wish you'd go and see him. I'll give you the address."

"I know of a very good elocutionist in Oxford Street. I think I would go and have some lessons, if I were you, Bruce; the summer classes are just beginning. They teach you to speak so clearly, to get your voice over the footlights, as it were. I think all men require to study oratory and elocution. It comes in so useful!"

Bruce lowered his voice almost to a whisper.

"Are you playing the fool with me?"

She nodded amiably in the manner of a person perfectly deaf, but who is pretending to hear.

"Yes, dear; yes, quite right."

"What do you mean by 'quite right'?" He unfastened his coat and threw it open, glaring at her a little.

"Who—me? *I* don't know."

"Who is that letter from, Edith?" he said breezily, in a tone of sudden careless and cheery interest.

"I haven't read it yet, Bruce," she answered, in the same tone, brightly.

"Oh. Why don't you read it?"

"Oh! I shall presently."

"When?"

"When I've opened it."

He took off his other glove, folded it with the first one, made them into a ball, and threw it across the room against the window, while his colour deepened.

"Oh, do you want to have a game? Shall I send for Archie?"

"Edith, why don't you take off your hat?"

"I can't think. Why don't you take off your coat?"

"I haven't time. Show me that letter."

"What letter?"

"Don't prevaricate with me." Bruce had now definitely lost his temper. "I can stand anything except prevarication. Anything in the world, but prevarication, I can endure, with patience. But *not* that! As if you didn't know perfectly well there's only one letter I want to see."

"Really?"

"Who's your letter from?"

"How should I know?"

Edith got up and went towards the door. Bruce was beforehand with her and barred the way, standing with his arms outstretched and his back to the door.

"Edith, I'm pained and surprised at your conduct!"

"Conduct!" she exclaimed.

"Don't echo my words! I will *not* be echoed, do you hear? . . . Behaviour, then, if you prefer the word. . . . Why don't you wish me to see that letter?"

Edith quickly looked at the letter. Until this moment she had had an unreasonable and nervous terror that Aylmer might have forgotten his intention of writing what he called officially, and might have written her what she now inwardly termed a lot of nonsense. But she now saw she had made a mistake: it was not his handwriting nor his postmark. She became firmer.

"Look here, Bruce," she said, in a decided voice, quietly. "We have been married eight years, and I consider you ought to trust me sufficiently to allow me to open my own letters."

"Oh, you do, do you? What next? What next! I suppose the next thing you'll wish is to be a suffragette."

"The question," said Edith, in the most cool, high, irritating voice she could command, "really, of votes for women hardly enters into our argument here. As a matter of fact, I take no interest in any kind of politics, and, I may be entirely wrong, but if I were compelled to take sides on the subject, I should be an anti-suffragist."

"Oh, you would, would you? That's as well to know! That's interesting. Give me that letter."

"Do you think you have the right to speak to me like that?"

"Edith," he said rather pathetically, trying to control himself. "I beg you, I *implore* you to let me see the letter! Hang it all! You know perfectly well, old girl, how fond I am of you. I may worry you a bit sometimes, but you know my heart's all right."

"Of course, Bruce; I'm not finding fault with you. I only want to read my own letter, that's all."

"But if I let you out of this room without having shown it me, then if there's something you don't want me to see, you'll tear it up or chuck it in the fire."

Edith was quite impressed at this flash of prophetic insight. She admitted to herself he was right.

"It's entirely a matter of principle," she said after another reassuring look at the envelope. "It's only a matter of principle, dear. I'm twenty-eight years old, we've been married eight years; you leave the housekeeping, the whole ordering of the children's education, and heaps of other quite important things, entirely to me; in fact, you lead almost the life of a schoolboy, without any of the tiresome part, and with freedom, going to school in the day and amusing yourself in the evening, while everything disagreeable and important is thought of and seen to for you. You only have the children with you when they amuse you. *I* have all the responsibility; I have to be patient, thoughtful—in fact, you leave things to me more than most men do to their wives, Bruce. You won't be bothered even to look at an account—to do a thing. But I'm not complaining."

"Oh, you're not! It sounded a little like it."

"But it isn't. I don't *mind* all this responsibility, but I ought, at least, to be allowed to read my letters."

"Well, darling, you shall, as a rule. Look here, old girl, you shall. I promise you, faithfully, dear. Oh, Edith, you're looking awfully pretty; I like that hat. Look here, I promise you, dear, I'll *never* ask you again, never as long as I live. But I've a fancy to read this particular letter. Why not just gratify it? It's a very harmless whim." His tone suddenly changed. "What do you suppose there's *in* the damned letter? Something you're jolly well anxious I shouldn't see."

She made a step forward. He rushed at her, snatched the letter out of her hand, and went to the window with it.

She went into her own room, shut the door, and threw herself on the bed, her whole frame shaking with suppressed laughter.

Bruce, alone, with trembling fingers tore open the envelope. Never in his life had he been opposed by Edith before in this way.

He read these words in stereotyped writing:

"Van will call on receipt of post-card. The Lavender Laundry hopes that you will give them a trial, as their terms are extremely mod——"

Bruce rushed to the door and called out:

"Edith! Sorry! Edie, I say, I'm sorry. Come back."

There was no answer.

He pushed the letter under the door of her room, and said through the keyhole:

"Edith, look here, I'm just going for a little walk. I'll be back to dinner. Don't be angry."

Bruce brought her home a large bunch of Parma violets. But neither of them ever referred to the question again, and for some time there was a little less of the refrain of "Am I master in my own house, or am I not?"

The next morning, when a long letter came from Aylmer, from Spain, Edith read it at breakfast and Bruce didn't ask a single question. However, she left it on his plate, as if by mistake. He might just as well read it.

CHAPTER XV

MAVIS ARGLES

VINCY had the reputation of spending his fortune with elaborate yet careful lavishness, buying nothing that he did not enjoy, and giving away everything he did not want. At the same time his friends occasionally wondered on what he *did* spend both his time and his money. He was immensely popular, quite sought after socially; but he declined half his invitations and lived a rather quiet existence in the small flat, with its Oriental decorations and violent post-impressions and fierce Chinese weapons, high up in Victoria Street. Vincy really concealed under an amiable and gentle exterior the kindest heart of any man in London. There was "more in him than met the eye," as people say, and, frank and confidential as he was to his really intimate friends, at least one side of his life was lived in shadow. It was his secret romance with a certain young girl artist, whom he saw rarely, for sufficient reasons. He was not devoted to her in the way that he was to Edith, for whom he had the whole-hearted enthusiasm of a loyal friend, and the idolising worship of a fanatic admirer It was perhaps Vincy's nature, a little, to sacrifice himself for anyone he was fond of. He spent a great deal of time thinking out means of helping materially the young art-student, and always he succeeded in this object by his elaborate and tactful care. For he knew she was very, very poor, and that her pride was of an old-fashioned order—she never said she was hard up, as every modern person does, whether rich or poor, but he knew that she really lacked what he considered very nearly—if not quite—the necessities of life.

Vincy's feeling for her was a curious one. He had known her since she was sixteen (she was now twenty-four). Yet he did not trust her, and she troubled him. He had met her at a studio at a time when he had thought of studying art seriously. Sometimes, something about her worried and wearied him, yet he couldn't do without her for long. The fact that he knew he was of great help to her fascinated him; he often thought that if she had been rich and he poor he would never wish to see her again. Certainly it was the touch of pathos in her life that held him; also, of course, she was pretty, with a pale thin face, deep blue eyes, and rich dark red frizzy hair that was always coming down—the untidy hair of the art-student.

He was very much afraid of compromising her, and *she* was very much afraid of the elderly aunt with whom she lived. She had no parents, which made her more pathetic, but no more free. He could not go and see her, with any satisfaction to either of them, at *her* home, though he did so occasionally. This was why she first went to see him at his flat. But these visits, as they were both placed, could, of course, happen rarely.

Mavis Argles—this was the girl's extraordinary name—had a curious fascination for him. He was rather fond of her, yet the greatest wish he had in the world was to break it off. When with her he felt himself to be at once a criminal and a benefactor, a sinner and a saint. Theoretically, theatrically, and perhaps conventionally, his relations with her constituted him the villain of the piece. Yet he behaved to her more like Don Quixote than Don Juan. . . .

One afternoon about four o'clock—he was expecting her—Vincy had arranged an elaborate tea on his little green marble dining-table.

Everything was there that she liked. She was particularly attached to scones; he also had cream-cakes, sandwiches, sweets, chocolate and strawberries. As he heard the well-known slightly creaking step, his heart began to beat loudly—quick beats. He changed colour, smiled, and nervously went to the door.

"Here you are, Mavis!" He calmed her and himself by this banal welcome.

He made a movement to help her off with her coat, but she stopped him, and he didn't insist, guessing that she supposed her blouse to be unfit for publication.

She sat down on the sofa, and leaned back, looking at him with her pretty, weary, dreary, young, blue eyes.

"It seems such a long time since I saw you," said Vincy. "You're tired; I wish I had a lift."

"I am tired," she spoke in rather a hoarse voice always. "And I ought not to stop long."

"Oh, stay a *minute* longer, won't you?" he asked.

"Well, I like that! I've only just this moment arrived!"

"Oh, Mavis, don't say that! Have some tea."

He waited on her till she looked brighter.

"How is Aunt Jessie?"

"Aunt Jessie's been rather ill."

"Still that nasty pain?" asked Vincy.

She stared at him, then laughed.

"As if you remember anything about it."

"Oh, Mavis! I do remember it. I remember what was the matter with her quite well."

"I bet you don't. What was it?" she asked, with childish eagerness.

"It was that wind round the heart that she gets sometimes. She told me about it. Nothing seems to shift it, either."

Mavis laughed—hoarse, childlike laughter that brought tears to her eyes.

"It's a shame to make fun of Aunt Jessie; she's a very, very good sort."

"Oh, good gracious, Mavis, if it comes to sorts, I'm sure she's quite at the top of the tree. But don't let's bother about her now."

"What *do* you want to bother about?"

"Couldn't you come out and dine with me, Mavis? It would be a change"—he was going to say "for you," but altered it—"for me."

"Oh no, Vincy; you can't take me out to dinner. I don't look up to the mark." She looked in a glass. "My hat—it's a very good hat—it cost more than you'd think—but it shows signs of wear."

"Oh, that reminds me," began Vincy. "What *do* you think happened the other day? A cousin of mine who was up in London a little while bought a hat—it didn't suit her, and she insisted on giving it to *me!* She didn't know what to do to get rid of it! I'd given her something or other, for her birthday, and *she* declared she would give this to *me* for *my* birthday, and so—I've got it on my hands."

"What a very queer thing! It doesn't sound true."

"No; does it? Do have some more tea, Mavis darling."

"No, thanks; I'll have another cake."

"May I smoke?"

She laughed. "Asking *me!* You do what you like in your own house."

"It's yours," he answered, "when you're here. And when you're not, even more," he added as an afterthought.

He struck a match; she laughed and said: "I don't believe I understand you a bit."

"Oh—I went to the play last night," said Vincy. "Oh, Mavis, it was such a wearing play."

"All about nothing, I suppose? They always are, now."

"Oh no. It was all about everything. The people were *so* clever; it was something cruel how clever they were. One man *did* lay down the law! Oh, didn't he though! I don't hold with being bullied and lectured from the stage, do you, Mavis? It seems so unfair when you can't answer back."

"Was it Bernard Shaw?" she asked.

"No; it wasn't; not this time; it was someone else. Oh, I do feel sometimes when I'm sitting in my stall, so good and quiet, holding my programme nicely and sitting up straight to the table, as it were, and then a fellow lets me have it, tells me where I'm wrong and all that; I *should* like to stand up and give a back answer, wouldn't you?"

"No; I'd like to see *you* do it! Er—what colour is that hat that your cousin gave you?"

"Oh, colour?" he said thoughtfully, smoking. "Let me see—what colour was it? It doesn't seem to me that it was any particular colour. It was a very curious colour. Sort of mole-colour. Or was it cerise? Or violet? . . . You wouldn't like to see it, would you?"

"Why, yes, I'd like to see it; I wouldn't try it on of course."

He opened the box.

"Why, what a jolly hat!" she exclaimed. "You may not know it, but that would just suit me; it would go with my dress, too."

"Fancy."

She took off her own hat, and touched up her hair with her fingers, and tried on the other. Under it her eyes brightened in front of the glass; her colour rose; she changed as one looked at her—she was sixteen again—the child he had first met at the Art School.

"Don't you think it suits me?" she said, turning round.

"Yes, I think you look very charming in it. Shall I put it back?"

There was a pause.

"I sha'n't know what on earth to do with it," he said discontentedly. "It's so silly having a hat about in a place like this. Of course you wouldn't care to keep it, I suppose? It does suit you all right, you know; it would be awfully kind of you."

"What a funny person you are, Vincy. I *should* like to keep it. What could I tell Aunt Jessie?"

"Ah, well, you see, that's where it is! I suppose it wouldn't do for you to tell her the truth."

"What do you mean by the truth?"

"I mean what I told you—how my cousin, Cissie Cavanack," he smiled a little as he invented this name, "came up to town, chose the wrong hat, didn't know what to do with it—and, you know!"

"I could tell her all that, of course."

"All right," said Vincy, putting the other hat—the old one—in the box. "Where shall we dine?"

"Oh, Vincy, I think you're very sweet to me, but how late dare I get back to Ravenscourt Park?"

"Why not miss the eight-five train?—then you'll catch the quarter to ten and get back at about eleven."

"Which would you *rather* I did?"

"Well, need you ask?"

"I don't know, Vincy. I have a curious feeling sometimes. I believe you're rather glad when I've gone—relieved!"

"Well, my dear," he answered, "look how you worry all the time! If you'd only have what I call a quiet set-down and a chat, without being always on the fidget, always looking either at the glass or at the clock, one might *not* have that feeling."

Her colour rose, and tears came to her eyes. "Oh, then you *are* glad when I'm gone!" She pouted. "You don't care for me a bit, Vincy," she said, in a plaintive voice.

He sat down next to her on the little striped sofa, and took her hand.

"Oh, give over, Mavis, do give over! I wish you wouldn't carry on like that; you do carry on, Mavis dear, don't you? Some days you go on something cruel, you do really. Reely, I mean. Now, cheer up and be jolly. Give a kiss to the pretty gentleman, and look at all these pretty good conduct stripes on the sofa! There! That's better."

"Don't speak as if I were a baby!"

"Do you mind telling me what we're quarrelling about, my dear? I only ask for information."

"Oh, we're *not*. You're awfully sweet. You know I love you, Vincy."

"I thought, perhaps, it was really all right."

"Sometimes I feel miserable and jealous."

He smiled. "Ah! What are you jealous of, Mavis?"

"Oh, everything—everyone—all the people you meet."

"Is that all? Well, you're the only person I ever meet—by appointment, at any rate."

"Well—the Ottleys!"

His eye instinctively travelled to a photograph of Edith, all tulle and roses; a rather fascinating portrait.

"What about *her?* asked Mavis. "What price Mrs. Ottley?"

"Really, Mavis!—What price? No price. Nothing about her; she's just a great friend of mine. I think I told you that before. ... What a frightfully bright light there is in the room," Vincy said. He got up and drew the blind down. He came back to her.

"Your hair's coming down," he remarked.

"I'm sorry," she said. "But at the back it generally is."

"Don't move—let me do it."

Pretending to arrange it, he took all the hairpins out, and the cloud of dark red hair fell down on her shoulders.

"I like your hair, Mavis."

"It seems too awful I should have been with you such a long time this afternoon," she exclaimed.

"It *isn't* long."

"And sometimes it seems so dreadful to think I can't be with you always."

"Yes, doesn't it? Mavis dear, will you do up your hair and come out to dinner?"

"Vincy dear, I think I'd better not, because of Aunt Jessie."

"Oh, very well; all right. Then you will another time."

"Oh, you don't want me to stay?"

"Yes, I do; do stay."

"No, next time—next Tuesday."

"Very well, very well."

He took a dark red carnation out of one of the vases and pinned it on to her coat.

"The next time I see you," she said, "I want to have a long, *long* talk."

"Oh yes; we must, mustn't we?"

He took her downstairs, put her into a cab. It was half-past six.

He felt something false, worrying, unreliable and incalculable in Mavis. She didn't seem real. . . . He wished she were fortunate and happy; but he wished even more that he were never going to see her again. And still! . . .

He walked a little way, then got into a taxi and drove to see Edith. When he was in this peculiar condition of mind—the odd mixture of self-reproach, satisfaction, amusement and boredom that he felt now—he always went to see Edith, throwing himself into the little affairs of her life as if he had nothing else on his mind. He was a little anxious about Edith. It seemed to him that since Aylmer had been away she had altered a little.

CHAPTER XVI

MORE OF THE MITCHELLS

EDITH had become an immense favourite with the Mitchells. They hardly ever had any entertainment without her. Her success with their friends delighted Mrs. Mitchell, who was not capable of commonplace feminine jealousy, and who regarded Edith as a find of her own. She often reproached Winthrop, her husband, for having known Bruce eight years without discovering his charming wife.

One evening they had a particularly gay party. Immediately after dinner Mitchell had insisted on dressing up, and was solemnly announced in his own house as Prince Gonoff, a Russian noble. He had a mania for disguising himself. He had once travelled five hundred miles under the name of Prince Gotoffski, in a fur coat, a foreign accent, a false moustache and a special saloon carriage. Indeed, only his wife knew all the secrets of Mitchell's wild early career of unpractical jokes, to some of which he still clung. When he was younger he had carried it pretty far. She encouraged him, yet at the same time she acted as ballast, and was always explaining his jokes; sometimes she was in danger of explaining him entirely away. She loved to tell of his earlier exploits. How often, when younger, he had collected money for charities (particularly for the Deaf and Dumb Cats' League, in which he took special interest), by painting halves of salmon and ships on fire on the cold grey pavement! Armed with an accordion, and masked to the eyes, he had appeared at Eastbourne, and also at the Henley Regatta, as a Mysterious Musician. At the regatta he had been warned off the course, to his great pride and joy. Mrs. Mitchell assured Edith that his bath-chair race with a few choice spirits was still talked of at St. Leonard's (bath-chairmen, of course, are put in the chairs, and you pull them along). Mr. Mitchell was beaten by a short head, but that, Mrs. Mitchell declared, was really most unfair, because he was so handicapped—his man was much stouter than any of the others—and the race, by rights, should have been run again.

When he was at Oxford he had been well known for concealing under a slightly rowdy exterior the highest spirits of any of the undergraduates. He was looked upon as the most fascinating of *farceurs*. It seems that he had distinguished himself there less for writing Greek verse, though he was good at it, than for the wonderful variety of fireworks that he persistently used to let off under the dean's window. It was this fancy of his that led, first, to his popularity, and afterwards to the unfortunate episode of his being sent down; soon after which he had married privately, chiefly in order to send his parents an announcement of his wedding in *The Morning Post*, as a surprise.

Some people had come in after dinner—for there was going to be a little *sauterie intime*, as Mrs. Mitchell called it, speaking in an accent of her own, so appalling that, as Vincy observed, it made it sound quite improper. Edith watched, intensely amused, as she saw that there were really one or two people present who, never having seen Mitchell before, naturally did not recognise him now, so that the disguise was considered a triumph. There was something truly agreeable in the deference he was showing to a peculiarly yellow lady in red, adorned with ugly real lace, and beautiful false hair. She was obviously delighted with the Russian prince.

"Winthrop is a wonderful man!" said Mrs.

Mitchell to Edith, as she watched her husband proudly. "Who would dream he was cleanshaven! Look at that moustache! Look at the wonderful way his coat doesn't fit; he's got just that Russian touch with his clothes; I don't know how he's done it, I'm sure. How I wish dear Aylmer Ross was here; he *would* appreciate it so much."

"Yes, I wish he were," said Edith.

"I can't think what he went away for. I suppose he heard the East a-calling, and all that sort of thing. The old wandering craving you read of came over him again, I suppose. Well, let's hope he'll meet some charming girl and bring her back as his bride. Where is he now, do you know, Mrs. Ottley?"

"In Armenia, I fancy," said Edith.

"Oh, well, we don't want him to bring home an Armenian, do we? What colour are they? Blue, or brown, or what? I hope no one will tell Lady Hartland that is my husband. She'll expect to see Winthrop, to-night; she never met him, you know; but he really ought to be introduced to her. I think I shall tell him to go and undress, when they've had a little dancing and she's been down to supper."

Lady Hartland was the yellow lady in red, who thought she was flirting with a fascinating Slav.

"She's a sort of celebrity," continued Mrs.

Mitchell. "She was an American once, and she married Sir Charles Hartland for her money. I hate these interested marriages, don't you? —especially when they're international. Sir Charles isn't here; he's such a sweet boy. He's a friend of Mr. Cricker; it's through Mr. Cricker I know them, really. Lady Everard has taken *such* a fancy to young Cricker; she won't leave him alone. After all he's *my* friend, and as he's not musical I don't see that she has any special right to him; but he's there every Wednesday now, and does his dances on their Sunday evenings too. He's got a new one—lovely, quite lovely—an imitation of Lydia Kyasht as a water-nymph. I wanted him to do it here to-night, but Lady Everard has taken him to the opera. Now, won't you dance? Your husband promised he would. You both look so young!"

Edith refused to dance. She sat in a corner with Vincy and watched the dancers.

By special permission, as it was so *intime*, the Turkey Trot was allowed. Bruce wanted to attempt it with Myra Mooney, but she was horrified, and insisted on dancing the 1880 *trois-temps* to a jerky American two-step.

"Edith," said Vincy; "I think you're quieter than you used to be. Sometimes you seem rather absent-minded."

"Am I? I'm sorry; there's nothing so tedious to other people. Why do you think I'm more serious?"

"I think you miss Aylmer."

"Yes, I do. He gave a sort of meaning to everything. He's always interesting. And there's something about him—I don't know what it is. Oh, don't be frightened, Vincy, I'm not going to use the word personality. Isn't that one of the words that ought to be forbidden altogether? In all novels and newspapers that poor, tired word is always cropping up."

"Yes, that and magnetism, and temperament, and technique. Let's cut out technique altogether. Don't let there be any, that's the best way; then no one can say anything about it. I'm fed up with it. Aren't you?"

"Oh, I don't agree with you at all. I think there ought to be any amount of technique, and personality, and magnetism, and temperament. I don't mind *how* much technique there is, as long as nobody talks about it. But neither of these expressions is quite so bad as that dreadful thing you always find in American books, and that lots of people have caught up—especially palmists and manicures—mentality."

"Yes, mentality's *very* depressing," said Vincy. "I could get along nicely without it,

I think. . . . I had a long letter from Aylmer to-day. He seemed unhappy."

"I had a few lines yesterday," said Edith. "He said he was having a very good time. What did he say to you?"

"Oh, he wrote frankly to *me*."

"Bored, is he?"

"Miserable; enamoured of sorrow; got the hump; frightfully off colour; wants to come back to London. He misses the Mitchells. I suppose it's the Mitchells."

Edith smiled and looked pleased. "He asked me not to come here much."

"Ah! But he wouldn't want you to go anywhere. That is so like Aylmer. He's not jealous, of course. How could he be? It's only a little exclusiveness. . . . And how delightfully rare that is, Edith dear. I admire him for it. Most people now seem to treasure anything they value in proportion to the extent that it's followed about and surrounded by the vulgar public. I sympathise with that feeling of wishing to keep—anything of that sort—to oneself."

"You are more secretive than jealous, yourself. But I have very much the same feeling," Edith said. "Many women I know think the ideal of happiness is to be in love with a great man, or to be the wife of a great public success;

to share his triumph! They forget you share the man as well!"

"I suppose the idea is that, after the publicity and the acclamation and the fame and the public glory and the shouting, you take the person home, and feel he is only yours, really."

"But, can a famous person be only yours? No. I shouldn't like it. It isn't that I don't *like* cleverness and brilliance, but I don't care for the public glory."

"I see; you don't mind how great a genius he is, as long as he isn't appreciated," replied Vincy. "Well, then, in heaven's name let us stick to our obscurities!"

CHAPTER XVII

THE AGONIES OF AYLMER

IN the fresh cheerfulness of the early morning, after sleep, with the hot June sun shining in at the window, Aylmer used to think he was better. He would read his letters and papers, dress slowly, look out of the window at the crowds on the pavement—he had come back to Paris—feel the infectious cheeriness and sense of adventure of the city; then he would say to himself that his trip had been successful. He *was* better. When he went out his heart began to sink a little already, but he fought it off; there would be a glimpse of an English face flashing past in a carriage—he thought of Edith, but he put it aside. Then came lunch. For some reason, immediately after lunch his malady—for, of course, such love *is* a malady—incongruously attacked him in an acute form. "Why after lunch?" he asked himself. Could it be that only when he was absolutely rested, before he had had any sort of fatigue, that the deceptive improvement would show itself? He felt a wondering humiliation at his own narrow grief.

However, this was the hour that it recurred; he didn't know why. He had tried all sorts of physical cures—for there is no disguising the fact that such suffering is physical, and so why should the cure not be, also? He had tried wine, no wine, exercise, distraction, everything—and especially a constant change of scene. This last was the worst of all. He felt so exiled in Sicily, and in Spain—so terribly far away—it was unbearable. He was happier directly he got to Paris, because he seemed more in touch with England and her. Yes; the pain *had* begun again. . . .

Aylmer went and sat alone outside the café. It was not his nature to dwell on his own sensations. He would diagnose them quickly and acutely, and then throw them aside. He was quickly bored with himself; he was no egotist. But to-day, he thought, he *would* analyse his state, to see what could be done.

Six weeks! He had not seen her for six weeks. The longing was no better. The pain seemed to begin at his throat, pressing down gradually on the chest. It was that feeling of oppression, he supposed, that makes one sigh; as though there were a weight on the heart. And certain little memories made it acute; sudden flashing vivid recollection of that last drive was like a sharp jagged tear. Had they ever been on nearer terms, and had she treated him badly, it would not have caused this slow and insidious suffering. He was a man of spirit; he was proud and energetic; he would have thrown it off. If he could have been angry with her, or despised her, he could have cured himself in time. Instead of that, all the recollections were of an almost sickening sweetness; particularly that kiss on the day he went to see her. And the other, the *second*, was also the last; so it had a greater bitterness.

> *"Rapture sharper than a sword,*
> *Joy like a sudden spear."*

These words, casually read somewhere, came back to him whenever he remembered her!

Aylmer had read, heard of these obsessions, but never believed in them. It was folly, madness!

He stood up, tossing his head as though to throw it off.

He went to fetch some friends, went with them to see pictures, to have tea, and to drive in the Bois, accepting also an invitation to dine with a man—a nice boy—a fellow who had been at Oxford with him, and was at the embassy here, a young attaché.

He was quite nice: a little dull, and a little too fond of talking about his chief.

Aylmer got home at about half-past six to dress for dinner. Then the torture began again. It was always worse towards evening—an agony of longing, regret, fury, vague jealousy and desire.

He stood and looked out of the window again at the crowd, hurrying along now to their pleasures or their happy homes. So many people in the world, like stars in the sky—why want the one star only? Why cry for the moon?

He had no photograph of her, but he still thought she was like his mother's miniature, and often looked at it. He wished he wasn't going to dine with that young man to-night. Aylmer was the most genial and sociable of men; he usually disliked being alone; yet just now being with people bored him; it seemed an interruption. He was going through a crisis.

Yes; he could not stand anyone this evening. He rang the bell and sent a *petit bleu* to say he was prevented from dining with his friend. What a relief when he had sent this—now he could think of her alone in peace. . . .

She had never asked him to go away. It was

his own idea. He had come away to get over it. Well, he hadn't got over it. He was worse. But it wasn't because he didn't see her; no, he didn't deceive himself. The more he saw of her the worse he would be. Not one man in a thousand was capable of feeling so intensely and deeply as Aylmer felt, and never in his life before had he felt anything like it. And now it came on again with the ebb and flow of passion, like an illness. Why was he so miserable—why would nothing else *do?* He suddenly remembered with a smile that when he was five years old he had adored a certain nurse, and for some reason or other his mother sent her away. He had cried and cried for her to come back. He remembered even now how people had said: "Oh, the child will soon forget." But he wore out their patience; he cried himself to sleep every night. And his perseverance had at last been rewarded. After six weeks the nurse came back. His mother sent for her in despair at the boy's misery. How well he remembered that evening and her plain brown face, with the twinkling eyes. How he kissed his mother, and thanked her! The nurse stayed till he went to school and then he soon forgot all about her. Perhaps it was in his nature at rare intervals to want one particular person so terribly, to pine and die for someone!

That was a recollection of babyhood, and yet he remembered even now that obstinate, aching longing. ... He suddenly felt angry, furious. What was Edith doing now? Saying good-night to Archie and Dilly? They certainly did look, as she had said, heavenly angels in their night attire (he had been privileged to see them). Then she was dressing for dinner and going out with Bruce. Good heavens! what noble action had Bruce ever done for *him* that he should go away? Why make such a sacrifice —for Bruce?

Perhaps, sometimes, she really missed him a little. They had had great fun together; she looked upon him as a friend; not only that, but he knew that he amused her, that she liked him, thought him clever, and—admired him even.

But that was all. Yet she *could* have cared for him. He knew that. And not only in one way, but in every way. They could have been comrades interested in the same things; they had the same sense of humour, much the same point of view. She would have made him, probably, self-restrained and patient as she was, in certain things. But, in others, wouldn't he have fired her with his own ideas and feelings, and violent passions and enthusiasms!

She was to be always with Bruce! That was to be her life!—Bruce, who was almost indescribable because he was neither bad, nor stupid, nor bad-looking. He had only one fault. "*Il n'a qu'un défaut—il est impossible,*" said Aylmer aloud to himself.

He took up a book—of course one of *her* books, something she had lent him.

Now it was time to go out again—to dinner. He couldn't; it was too much effort. To-night he would give way, and suffer grief and desire and longing like a physical pain. He hadn't heard from her lately. Suppose she should be ill? Suppose she was forgetting him entirely? Soon they would be going away to some summer place with the children. He stamped his foot like an angry child as he imagined her in her thin summer clothes. How people would admire her! How young she would look! Why couldn't he find some fault with her?—imagine her cold, priggish, dull, too cautious. But he could only think of her as lovely, as beyond expression attractive, drawing him like a magnet, as marvellously kind, gentle, graceful, and clever. He was obliged to use the stupid word clever, as there was no other. He suddenly remembered her teeth when she smiled, and a certain slight wave in her thick hair that was a natural one. It is really barely decent to write about poor Aylmer as he is alone, suffering, thinking himself unwatched. He suddenly threw himself on his bed and gave way to a crisis of despair.

About an hour later, when the pain had somehow become stupefied, he lit a cigarette, ashamed of his emotion even to himself, and rang. The servant brought him a letter—the English post.

He had thought so much of her, felt her so deeply the last few days that he fancied it must somehow have reached her. He read:

"MY DEAR AYLMER,—I'm glad you are in Paris; it seems nearer home. Last night I went to the Mitchells' and Mr. Mitchell disguised himself as a Russian Count. Nobody worried about it, and then he went and undisguised himself again. But Lady Hartland worried about it, and as she didn't know the Mitchells before, when he was introduced to her properly she begged him to give her the address of that charming Russian. And Vincy was there, and darling Vincy told me you'd written him a letter saying you weren't so very happy. And oh, Aylmer, I don't see the point of your waiting till September to come back. Why don't you come *now*?

"We're going away for Archie's holidays.

Come back and see us and take Freddie with us somewhere in England. You told me to ask you when I wanted you—ask you anything I wanted. Well, I want to see you. I miss you too much. You arrived in Paris last night. Let me know when you can come. I want you.
                                                EDITH."

The bell was rung violently. Orders were given, arrangements made, packing was done. Aylmer was suddenly quite well, quite happy.

In a few hours he was in the midnight express due to arrive in London at six in the morning—happy beyond expression.

By ten o'clock in the morning he would hear her voice on the telephone.

He met a poor man just outside the hotel selling matches, in rags. Aylmer gave him three hundred francs. He pretended to himself that he didn't want any more French money. He felt he wanted someone else to be happy too.

CHAPTER XVIII

A CONTRETEMPS

EDITH did not know, herself, what had induced her to write that letter to Paris. Some gradual obscure influence, in an impulsive moment of weakness, a conventional dread of Paris for one's idol. Then, what Vincy told her had convinced her Aylmer was unhappy. She thought that surely there might be some compromise; that matters could be adjusted. Couldn't they go on seeing each other just as friends? Surely both would be happier than separated? For, yes—there was no doubt she missed him, and longed to see him. Is there any woman in the world on whom a sincere declaration from a charming, interesting person doesn't make an impression, and particularly if that person goes away practically the next day, leaving a blank? Edith had a high opinion of her own strength of will. When she appeared weak it was on some subject about which she was indifferent. She took a great pride in her own self-poise; her self-control, which was neither coldness nor density. She had made up her mind to bear always with the little irritations Bruce caused her; to guide him in the right direction; keep her influence with him in order to be able to arrange everything about the children just as *she* wished. The children were a deep and intense preoccupation. To say she adored them is insufficient. Archie she regarded almost as her greatest friend, Dilly as a pet; for both she had the strongest feeling that a mother could have. And yet the fact remained that they did not nearly fill her life. With Edith's intellect and temperament they could only fill a part.

Bending down to a lower stature of intelligence all day long would make one's head ache; standing on tiptoe and stretching up would do the same; one needs a contemporary and a comrade.

Perhaps till Edith met Aylmer she had not quite realised what such real comradeship might mean, coupled with another feeling—not the intellectual sympathy she had for Vincy, but something quite different. When she recollected their last drive her heart beat quickly, and the little memories of the few weeks of their friendship gave her unwonted moments of sentiment.

Above all, it was a real, solid happiness—an uplifting pleasure, to believe he was utterly devoted to her. And so, in a moment of depression, a feeling of the sense of the futility of her life, she had, perhaps a little wantonly, written to ask him to come back. It is human to play with what one loves.

She thought she had a soft, tender admiration for him; that he had a charm for her; that she admired him. But she had not the slightest idea that on her side there was anything that could disturb her in any way. And so that his sentiment, which she had found to be rather infectious, should never carry her away, she meant only to see him now and then; to meet again and be friends.

As soon as she had written the letter and sent it she felt again a cheerful excitement. She felt sure he would come in a day or two.

Aylmer arrived, as I have said, eight hours after he received the letter. His first intention was to ring her up, or to speak to Bruce on the telephone. But it so happened that it was engaged. This decided him to have a short rest, and then go and surprise her with a visit. He thought he would have lunch at one (he knew she always lunched with the

A CONTRETEMPS 171

children at this hour), and would call on her unexpectedly at two, before she would have time to go out. They might have a long talk; he would give her the books and things he had bought for her, and he would have the pleasure of surprising her and seeing on her face that first look that no one can disguise, the look of real welcome.

Merely to be back in the same town made him nearly wild with joy. How jolly London looked at the beginning of July! So gay, so full of life. And then he read a letter in a writing he didn't know; it was from Mavis Argles, the friend of Vincy—the young art-student: Vincy had given her his address some time ago —asking him for some special privilege which he possessed, to see some of the Chinese pictures in the British Museum. He was to oblige her with a letter to the museum. She would call for it. Vincy was away, and evidently she had by accident chosen the day of Aylmer's return without knowing anything of his absence. She had never seen him in her life.

Aylmer was wandering about the half-dismantled house *désœuvré*, with nothing to do, restlessly counting the minutes till two in the afternoon. He remembered the very little that Vincy had told him of Mavis; how proud she was and how hard up. He saw her through the window. She looked pale and rather shabby. He told the servant to show her in.

"I've just this moment got your letter, Miss Argles. But, of course, I'm only too delighted."

"Thank you. Mr. Vincy said you'd give me the letter."

The girl sat down stiffly on the edge of a chair. Vincy had said she was pretty. Aylmer could not see it. But he felt brimming over with sympathy and kindness for her—for everyone, in fact.

She wore a thin light grey cotton dress, and a small grey hat; her hair looked rich, red, and fluffy as ever; her face white and rather thin. She looked about seventeen. When she smiled she was pretty; she had a Rossetti mouth; that must have been what Vincy admired. Aylmer had no idea that Vincy did more than admire her very mildly.

"Won't you let me take you there?" suggested Aylmer suddenly. He had nothing on earth to do, and thought it would fill up the time. "Yes! I'll drive you there and show you the pictures. And then, wouldn't you come and have lunch? I've got an appointment at two."

She firmly declined lunch, but consented that he should drive her, and they went.

A CONTRETEMPS 173

Aylmer talked with the eagerness produced by his restless excitement and she listened with interest, somewhat fascinated, as people always were, with his warmth and vitality.

As they were driving along Oxford Street Edith, walking with Archie, saw them clearly. She had been taking him on some mission of clothes. (For the children only she went into shops.) He was talking with such animation that he did not see her, to a pale young girl with bright red hair. Edith knew the girl by sight, knew perfectly well that she was Vincy's friend—there was a photograph of her at his rooms. Aylmer did not see her. After a start she kept it to herself. She walked a few steps, then got into a cab. She felt ill.

So Aylmer had never got her letter? He had been in London without telling her. He had forgotten her. Perhaps he was deceiving her? And he was making love obviously to that sickening, irritating red-haired fool (so Edith thought of her), Vincy's silly, affected artstudent.

When Edith went home she had a bad quarter of an hour. She never even asked herself what right she had to mind so much; she only knew it hurt. A messenger boy at once, of course.

"Dear Mr. Ross,—I saw you this morning. I wrote you a line to Paris, not knowing you had returned. When you get the note forwarded, will you do me the little favour to tear it up unopened? I'm sure you will do this to please me.

"We are going away in a day or two, but I don't know where. Please don't trouble to come and see me.

"Good-bye.

"Edith Ottley."

Aylmer left Miss Argles at the British Museum. When he went back, he found this letter.

CHAPTER XIX

AN EXTRAORDINARY AFTERNOON

AYLMER guessed at once she had seen him driving. Being a man of sense, and not an impossible hero in a feuilleton, instead of going away again and leaving the misunderstanding to ripen, he went to the telephone, endeavoured to get on, and to explain, in few words, what had obviously happened. To follow the explanation by an immediate visit was his plan. Though, of course, slightly irritated that she had seen him under circumstances conveying a false impression, on the other hand he was delighted at the pique her letter showed, especially coming immediately after the almost tender letter in Paris.

He rang and rang (and used language), and after much difficulty getting an answer he asked, *"Why he could not get on,"* a pathetic question asked plaintively by many people (not only on the telephone).

"The line is out of order."

In about twenty minutes he was at her door. The lift seemed to him preternaturally slow.

"Mrs. Ottley?"

"Mrs. Ottley is not at home, sir."

At his blank expression the servant, who knew him, and of course liked him, as they always did, offered the further information that Mrs. Ottley had gone out for the whole afternoon.

"Are the children at home, or out with Miss Townsend?"

"The children are out, sir, but not with Miss Townsend. They are spending the day with their grandmother."

"Oh! Do you happen to know if Mr. and Mrs. Ottley will be at home to dinner?"

"I've heard nothing to the contrary, sir."

"May I come in and write a note?"

He went into the little drawing-room. It was intensely associated with her. He felt a little *ému.* . . . There was the writing-table, there the bookcase, the few chairs, the grey walls; some pale roses fading in a pewter vase. . . . The restfulness of the surroundings filled him, and feeling happier he wrote on the grey notepaper:

"DEAR MRS. OTTLEY, — I arrived early this morning. I started, in fact, from Paris immediately after receiving a few lines you very kindly sent me there. I'm so disappointed not to see you. Unless I hear to the contrary—and even if I do, I think!—I propose to come round this evening about nine, and tell you and Bruce all about my travels.

"Excuse my country manners in thus inviting myself. But I know you will say no if you don't want me. And in that case I shall have to come another time, very soon, instead, as I really must see you and show you something I've got for Archie. Yours always——"

He paused, and then added:

"Sincerely,
"AYLMER ROSS."

He went to his club, there to try and pass the time until the evening. He meant to go in the evening, even if she put him off again; and, if they were out, to wait until they returned, pretending he had not heard from her again.

He was no better. He had been away six weeks and was rather more in love than ever. He would only see her—she *did* want to see him before they all separated for the summer! He could not think further than of the immediate future; he would see her; they could make plans afterwards. Of course, her letter was simply pique! She had given herself away—twice—once in the angry letter, also in the previous one to Paris. Where was she now? What did it mean? Why did she go out for the whole afternoon? Where was she?

. . . .

After Edith had written and sent her letter to Aylmer in the morning, Mrs. Ottley the elder came to fetch the children to dine, and Edith told Miss Townsend to go for the afternoon. She was glad she would be absolutely alone.

"Aren't you very well, dear Mrs. Ottley?" asked this young lady, in her sweet, sympathetic way.

Edith was fond of her, and, by implication only, occasionally confided in her on other subjects than the children. To-day, however, Edith answered that she was *very* well *indeed*, but was going to see about things before they went away. "I don't know how we shall manage without you for the holidays, Miss Townsend. I think you had better come with us for the first fortnight, if you don't mind much."

Miss Townsend said she would do whatever Edith liked. She could easily arrange to go with them at once. This was a relief, for just at this moment Edith felt as if even the children would be a burden.

Sweet, gentle Miss Townsend went away.

AN EXTRAORDINARY AFTERNOON 179

She was dressed rather like herself, Edith observed; she imitated Edith. She had the soft, graceful manner and sweet voice of her employer. She was slim and had a pretty figure, but was entirely without Edith's charm or beauty. Vaguely Edith wondered if she would ever have a love affair, ever marry. She hoped so, but (selfishly) not till Archie went to Eton.

Then she found herself looking at her lonely lunch; she tried to eat, gave it up, asked for a cup of tea.

At last, she could bear the flat no longer. It was a glorious day, very hot. Edith felt peculiar. She thought that if she spent all the afternoon out and alone, it would comfort her, and she would think it out. Trees and sky and sun had always a soothing effect on her. She went out, walked a little, felt worried by the crowd of shoppers swarming to Sloane Street and the Brompton Road, got into a taxi and drove to the gate of Kensington Gardens, opposite Kensington Gore. Here she soon found a seat. At this time of the day the gardens were rather unoccupied, and in the burning July afternoon she felt almost as if in the country. She took off her gloves—a gesture habitual with her whenever possible. She looked utterly restful. She had nothing in her hands, for she never carried either a parasol or a bag, nor even in winter a muff or in the evening a fan. All these little accessories seemed unnecessary to her. She liked to simplify. She hated fuss, anything worrying, agitating.

. . . And now she felt deeply, miserable perturbed and agitated. What a punishment for giving way to that half-coquettish, half self-indulgent impulse that had made her write to Paris! She had begged him to come back; while, really, he was here, and had not even let her know. She had never liked what she had heard of Mavis Argles, but had vaguely pitied her, wondering what Vincy saw in her, and wishing to believe the best. *Now*, she assumed the worst! As soon as Vincy had gone out of town—he was staying in Surrey with some of his relatives—*she*, the minx, began flirting or carrying on with Aylmer. How far had it gone? she wondered jealously. She did not believe Aylmer's love-making to be harmless. He was so easily carried away. His feelings were impulsive. Yet it was only a very short time since Vincy had told her of Aylmer's miserable letter. Edith was not interested in herself, and seldom thought much of her own feelings, but she hated self-deception; and now she faced facts. She adored

Aylmer! It had been purely jealousy that made her write to Paris so touchingly, asking him to come back—vague fears that, if he were so depressed in Spain, perhaps he might try by amusements to forget her in Paris. He had once said to her that, of all places, he thought Paris the least attractive for a romance, because it was all so obvious, so prepared, so professional. He liked the unexpected, the veiled and somewhat more hypocritical atmosphere, and in the fogs of London, he had said, were more romantic mysteries than in any other city. Still, she had feared. And besides she longed to see him. So she had unbent and thought herself soon after somewhat reckless; it was a little wanton and unfair to bring him back. But she was not a saint; she was a woman; and sometimes Bruce was trying. . . .

Edith belonged to the superior class of human being whom jealousy chills and cures, and does not stimulate to further efforts. It was not in her to go in for competition. The moment she believed someone else took her place she relaxed her hold. This is the finer temperament, but it suffers most.

She would not try to take Aylmer away. Let him remain with his red-haired Miss Argles! He might even marry her. He deserved it.

She meant to tell Vincy, of course. Poor Vincy, *he* didn't know of the treachery.

Now she must devote herself to the children, and be good and kind to Bruce. At least, Bruce was *true* to her in his way.

He had been in love when they married, but Edith shrewdly suspected he was not capable of very much more than a weak rather fatuous sentiment for any woman. And anyone but herself would have lost him many years ago, would very likely have given him up. But she had kept it all together, had really helped him, and was touched when she remembered that jealous scene he made about the letter. The letter she wouldn't at first let him see. Poor Bruce! Well, they were linked together. There were Archie, the angel, and Dilly, the pet. . . . She was twenty-eight and Aylmer forty. He ought not to hold so strong a position in her mind. But he did. Yes, she was in love with him in a way—it was a mania, an obsession. But she would now soon wrestle with it and conquer it. The great charm had been his exclusive devotion—but also his appearance, his figure, his voice. He looked sunburnt and handsome. He was laughing as he talked to the miserable creature (so Edith called her in her own mind).

AN EXTRAORDINARY AFTERNOON 183

Then Edith had a reaction. She would cure herself to-day! No more flirtation, no more *amitié amoureuse*. They were going away. The children, darlings, how they loved her! And Bruce. She was reminding herself she must be gentle, good, to Bruce. He had at least never deceived her!

She got up and walked on and on. It was about five o'clock now. As she walked, she thought how fortunate she was in Miss Townsend; what a nice girl she was, what a good friend to her and the children. She had a sort of intuition that made her always have the right word, the right manner. She had seemed a little odd lately, but she was quite pleased to come with them to the country. What made her think of Miss Townsend? Some way off was a girl, with her back to Edith, walking with a man. Her figure was like Miss Townsend's, and she wore a dress like the one copied from Edith's. Edith walked more quickly, it was the retired part of the gardens on the way towards the Bayswater Road. The two figures turned down a flowery path. . . . It was Miss Townsend! She had turned her face. Edith was surprised, was interested, and walked on a few steps. She had not seen the man clearly. Then they both sat down on a seat. He took her hand. She left it in his. There was something familiar in his figure and clothes, and Edith saw his face.

Yes, it was Bruce.

Edith turned round and went home.

CHAPTER XX

JOURNEYS END

SO that was how Bruce behaved to her!

The deceit of both of them hurt her immensely. But she pulled herself together. It was a case for action. She felt a bitter, amused contempt, but she felt it half-urgent *not* to do anything that would lead to a life of miserable bickering and mutual harm.

It must be stopped. And without making Bruce hate her.

She wrote the second note of this strange day and sent it by a messenger.

Giving no reason of any kind, she told the governess that she had decided the children's holidays should begin from that day, and that she was unexpectedly going away with them almost immediately, and she added that she would not require Miss Townsend any more. She enclosed a cheque, and said she would send on some books and small possessions that Miss Townsend had kept there.

This was sent by a messenger to Miss Townsend's home near Westbourne Grove. She would find it on her return from her walk!

And now Edith read Aylmer's note—it was so real, so sincere, she began to disbelieve her eyes this morning.

It gave her more courage; she wanted to be absolutely calm, and looking her very best, for Bruce's entrance.

He came in with his key. He avoided her eye a little—looked rather sheepish, she thought. It was about seven.

"Hallo! Aren't the children in yet? Far too late for them to be out."

"Nurse fetched Dilly. She has gone to bed. Archie is coming presently; mother will send him all right."

"How are you, Edith, old girl?"

"I'm quite well, Bruce."

"I have a sort of idea, as you know," he said, growing more at ease, "that we shall rather miss—a—Miss Townsend, when we first go away. What do you think of taking her for part of the time?"

"Dinner's ready," announced Edith, and they dined. Towards the end of dinner he was about to make the suggestion again, when Edith said in clear, calm but decided tones:

"Bruce, I am not going to take Miss Townsend away with us. She is not coming any more."

"Not—— Why? What the devil's the idea of this new scheme? What's the matter with Miss Townsend?"

"Bruce," answered Edith, "I prefer not to go into the question, and later you will be glad I did not. I've decided that Miss Townsend is not to come any more at all. I've written to tell her so. I'll look after the children with nurse until we come back. . . . It's all settled."

Bruce was silent.

"Well upon my word!" he exclaimed, looking at her uneasily. "Have it your own way, of course—but upon my word! Why?"

"Do you really want me to tell you exactly why? I would so much prefer not."

"Oh, all right, Edith dear; after all—hang it all—you're the children's mother—it's for you to settle. . . . No, I don't want to know anything. Have it as you wish."

"Then we won't discuss it again. Shall we?"

"All right."

He was looking really rather shamefaced, and she thought she saw a gleam of remorse and also of relief in his eye. She went into the other room. She had not shown him Aylmer's letter.

After ten minutes he came in and said: "Look here, Edith. Make what arrangements you like. *I* never want to see—Miss Townsend again."

She looked a question.

"And I never shall."

She was really pleased at this, and held out her hand. Bruce had tears in his eyes as he took it.

"Edith, old girl, I think I'll go round to the club for an hour or two."

"Do. And look here, Bruce, leave it to me to tell the children. They'll forget after the holidays. Archie must not be upset."

"Whatever you do, Edith, will be—— What I mean to say is that—— Well, good-night; I sha'n't be long."

Edith was really delighted, she felt she had won, and she *did* want that horrid little Townsend to be scored off! Wasn't it natural? She wanted to hear no more about it.

There was a ring. It was nine o'clock. It was Aylmer's voice.

CHAPTER XXI

THE GREAT EXCEPTION

THE absurdly simple explanation, made almost in dumb show, by action rather than in dialogue, was soon given. He was surprised, simply enchanted, at the entire frankness of her recognition; she acknowledged openly that it mattered to her tremendously whether or not he was on intimate terms or flirting with little Miss Argles, or with little Miss anybody. He was not even to look at any woman except herself, that was arranged between them now and understood. They were side by side, with hands clasped as a matter of course, things taken for granted that he formerly never dreamt of. The signs of emotion in her face he attributed of course to the morning's contretemps, knowing nothing of the other trouble.

"It's heavenly being here again. You're prettier than ever, Edith; sweeter than ever.

What a time I had away. It got worse and worse."

"Dear Aylmer!"

"You're far too good and kind to me. But I *have* suffered—awfully."

"So have I, since this morning. I felt——"

"What did you feel? Tell me!"

"Must I?"

"Yes!"

"I felt, when I saw you with her, as if I hadn't got a friend in the world. I felt quite alone. I felt as if the ground were going to open and swallow me up. I relied on you so much, far more than I knew! I was struck dumb, and rooted to the spot, and knocked all of a heap, in a manner of speaking, as Vincy would say," Edith went on, laughing. "But now, you've cured me thoroughly; you're such a *real* person."

"Angel!"

She still left her hand in his. Her eyes were very bright, the result of few but salt tears, the corners of her mouth were lifted by a happy smile, not the tantalising, half-mocking smile he used to see. She was changed, and was, he thought, more lovable—prettier; to-day's emotion had shaken her out of herself. The reaction of this evening gave a brilliancy to her eyes, happy curves to her lips, and the slight disarrangement of her hair, not quite silky-smooth to-night, gave her a more irresponsible look. She seemed more careless—younger.

"Where's Bruce?" Aylmer asked suddenly.

"He's gone to the club. He'll be back rather soon, I should think."

"I won't wait. I would rather not meet him this evening. When shall I see you again?"

"Oh, I don't know. I don't think I want to make any plans now."

"As you wish. I say, do you really think Vincy can care for that girl?"

"I believe he has had a very long friendship of some kind with her. He's never told me actually, but I've felt it," Edith said.

"Is he in love with her? Can he be?"

"In a way—in one of his peculiar ways."

"She's in love with him, I suppose," said Aylmer. "It was only because she thought it would please him that she wanted to see those things at the museum. I think she's a little anxious. I found her a wild, irritating, unaccountable, empty creature. I believe she wants him to marry her."

"I hope he won't, unless he *really* wants to," said Edith. "It would be a mistake for Vincy to sacrifice himself as much as that."

"I hope indeed he won't," exclaimed Aylmer. "And I think it's out of the question. Miss Argles is only an incident, surely. She looks the slightest of episodes."

"It's a very long episode. It might end, though—if she insists and he won't."

"Oh, bother, never mind them!" Aylmer replied, with boyish impatience. "Let me look at *you* again. Do you care for me a little bit, Edith?"

"Yes; I do."

"Well, what's going to be done about it?" he asked, with happy triviality.

"Don't talk nonsense," she replied. "We're just going to see each other sometimes."

"I'll be satisfied with anything!" cried Aylmer, "after what I've suffered not seeing you at all. We'll have a new game. You shall *make* the rules and I'll keep them."

"Naturally."

"About the summer?"

"Oh, no plans to-night. I must think." She looked thoughtful.

"Tell me, how's Archie?" he said.

"Archie's all right—delightful. Dilly, too. But I'm rather bothered."

"Why should you bother? What's it about? Tell me at once."

She paused a moment. "Miss Townsend

won't be able to come back any more," she said steadily.

"Really? What a pity. I suppose the fool of a girl's engaged, or something."

"She won't come back any more," answered Edith.

"Will you have to get a new Miss Townsend?"

"I thought of being their governess myself—during the holidays, anyhow."

"But that will leave you hardly any time—no leisure."

"Leisure for what?"

"For anything—for me, for instance," said Aylmer boldly. He was full of the courage and audacity caused by the immense relief of seeing her again and finding her so responsive.

There is, of course, no joy so great as the cessation of pain; in fact all joy, active or passive, *is* the cessation of some pain, since it must be the satisfaction of a longing, even perhaps an unconscious longing. A desire is a sort of pain, even with hope, without it is despair. When, for example, one takes artistic pleasure in looking at something beautiful, that is a cessation of the pain of having been deprived of it until then, since what one enjoys one must have longed for even without knowing it.

"Look here," said Aylmer suddenly, "I don't believe I can do without you."

"You said *I* was to make the rules."

"Make them then; go on."

"Well, we'll be intimate friends, and meet as often as we can. Once a week you may say you care for me, and I'll say the same. That's all. If you find you don't like it—can't stand it, as you say—then you'll have to go away again."

"I agree to it all, to every word. You'll see if I don't stick to it absolutely."

"Thank you, dear Aylmer."

He paused.

"Then I mustn't kiss you?"

"No. Never again."

"All right. Never again after to-night. To-night is the great exception," said Aylmer.

She made a tardy and futile protest. Then she said:

"Now, Aylmer, you must go." She sighed. "I have a lot of worries."

"I never heard you say that before. Let me take them and demolish them for you. Can't you give them to me?"

"No; I shall give nothing more to you. Good-bye. . . .

"Remember, there are to be no more exceptions," said Edith.

"I promise."

She sat quietly alone for half-an-hour, waiting for Bruce.

She now felt sorry for Bruce, utterly and completely indifferent about "the Townsend case," as she already humorously called it to herself. But, she thought, she *must* be strong! She was not prepared to lose her dignity, nor to allow the children to be educated by a woman whose faith at least with them and in their home was unreliable; their surroundings must be crystal-clear. It would make a certain difference to them, she thought. How could it not? There were so many little ways in which she might spoil them or tease them, scamp things, or rush them, or be nicer to one of them, or less nice, if she had any sort of concealed relation with their father. And as she had been treated absolutely as a confidante by Edith, the girl had certainly shown herself treacherous, and rather too clearly capable of dissimulation. Edith thought this must have a bad effect on the children.

Edith was essentially a very feminine woman though she had a mental attitude rightly held to be more characteristic of men. Being so feminine, so enraged under her calm and ease, she was, of course, not completely consistent. She was still angry, and very scornful of Miss Townsend. She was hurt with her; she felt a friend had played her false—a friend, too, in the position of deepest trust, of grave responsibility. Miss Townsend knew perfectly well what the children were to Edith, and, for all she knew, there was no one in Edith's life except Bruce; so that it was rather cruel. Edith intended to keep up her dignity so absolutely that Miss Townsend could never see her again, that she could never speak to Edith on the subject. She wished also, *very* much, that Bruce should never see her again, but didn't know how to encompass this. She must find a way.

On the other hand, after the first shock and disgust at seeing him, Edith's anger with Bruce himself had entirely passed. Had she not known, for years, that he was a little weak, a little fatuous? He was just as good a sort now as he had ever been, and as she was not blinded by the resentment and fury of the real jealousy of passion, Edith saw clearly, and knew that Bruce cared far more for *her* than for anybody else; that in so far as he could love anybody he loved her in his way. And she wanted to keep the whole thing together on account of Archie, and for Dilly's sake. She must be so kind, yet so strong that Bruce would be at once grateful for her forbearance and afraid to take advantage of it. Rather a difficult undertaking! . . .

And she had seen Aylmer again! There was nothing in it about Miss Argles. What happiness! She ought to have trusted him. He cared for her. He loved her. His sentiment was worth having. And she cared for him too; how much she didn't quite know. She admired him; he fascinated her, and she also felt a deep gratitude because he gave her just the sort of passionate worship that she must have always unconsciously craved for.

Certainly the two little events of to-day had drawn her nearer to him. She had been far less reserved that evening. She closed her eyes and smiled to herself. But this mustn't happen again.

With a strong effort of self-coercion she banished all delightful recollections as she heard Bruce come up in the lift.

He came in with a slightly shy, uncomfortable manner. Again, she felt sorry for him.

"Hallo!" he said.

He gave her a quick glance, a sort of cautious look which made her feel rather inclined to laugh. Then he said:

"I've just been down to the club. What have you been doing?"

"Aylmer's been here."

"Didn't know he was in town."

"He's only come for a few days."

"I should like to see him," said Bruce, looking brighter. "Did he ask after me?"

"Yes."

He looked at her again and said suspiciously:

"I suppose you didn't mention——"

"Mention what?"

"Edith!"

"Yes?"

He cleared his throat and then said with an effort of self-assertion that she thought at once ridiculous and touching:

"Look here, I don't wish to blame you in any way for what—er—arrangements you like to make in your own household. But—er—have you written to Miss Townsend?"

"Yes; she won't come back."

"Er—but won't she ask why?"

"I hope not."

"Why?" asked Bruce, with a tinge of defiance.

"Because then I should have to explain. And I don't like explaining."

There was another pause. Bruce seemed to take a great interest in his nails, which he examined separately one at a time, and then all together, holding both hands in front of him.

"Did Archie enjoy his day?"

"Oh yes," said Edith.

Bruce suddenly stood up, and a franker, more manly expression came into his face. He looked at her with a look of pain. Tears were not far from his eyes.

"Edith, you're a brick. You're too good for me."

She looked down and away without answering.

"Look here, is there anything I can do to please you?"

"Yes, there is."

"What? I'll do it, whatever it is, on my word of honour."

"Well, it's a funny thing to ask you, but you know our late governess, Miss Townsend? I should like you to promise never to see her again, even by accident. If you meet her—by accident, I mean—I want you not to see her."

Bruce held out both his hands.

"I swear I'd never recognise her even if I should meet her accidentally."

"I know it's a very odd thing to ask," continued Edith, "just a fancy; why should I mind your not seeing Miss Townsend?"

He didn't answer.

"However, I *do* mind, and I'll be grateful."

Edith thought one might be unfaithful without being disloyal, and she believed Bruce now. She was too sensible to ask him never to write a line, never to telephone, never to do anything else; besides, it was beneath her dignity to go into these details, and common-sense told her that one or the other must write or communicate if the thing was to be stopped. If Miss Townsend wrote to him to the club, he would have to answer. Bruce meant not to see her again, and that was enough.

"Then you're not cross, Edith—not depressed?"

She gave her sweetest smile. She looked brilliantly happy and particularly pretty.

"Edith!"

With a violent reaction of remorse, and a sort of tenderness, he tried to put his arm round her. She moved away.

"Don't you forgive me, Edith, for anything I've done that you don't like?"

"Yes, I *entirely* forgive you. The incident is closed."

"Really forgive me?"

"Absolutely. And I've had a tiring day and I'm going to sleep. Good-night."

With a kind little nod she left him standing

in the middle of the room, with that air of stupid distinction that he generally assumed when in a lift with other people, and that came to his rescue at awkward moments—a dull, aloof, rather haughty expression. But it was no use to him now.

He had considerable difficulty in refraining from venting his temper on the poor, dumb furniture; in fact, he did give a kick to a pretty little writing-table. It made no sound, but its curved shoulder looked resentful.

"What a day!" said Bruce to himself.

He went to his room, pouting like Archie. But he knew he had got off cheaply.

CHAPTER XXII

ANOTHER SIDE OF BRUCE

EVER since his earliest youth, Bruce had always had, at intervals, some vague, vain, half-hearted entanglement with a woman. The slightest interest, practically even common civility, shown him by anyone of the feminine sex between the ages of sixteen and sixty, flattered his vanity to such an extraordinary extent that he immediately thought these ladies were in love with him, and it didn't take much more for him to be in love with them. And yet he didn't really care for women. With regard to them his point of view was entirely that of vanity, and in fact he only liked both men or women who made up to him, or who gave him the impression that they did. Edith was really the only woman for whom his weak and flickering passion had lingered at all long; and in addition to that (the first glamour of which had faded) she had a real hold over him. He felt for her the most genuine fondness of which he was capable, besides trust and a certain admiration. A sort of respect underlay all his patronising good-nature or caprices with her. But still he had got into the habit of some feeble flirtation, a little affair, and at first he missed it very much. He didn't care a straw for Miss Townsend; he never had. He thought her plain and tedious; she bored him more than any woman he had ever met, and yet he had slipped into a silly sort of intrigue, beginning by a few words of pity or sympathy to her, and by the idea that she looked up to him in admiration. He was very much ashamed of it and of the circumstances; he was not proud of his conquest with her, as he generally was. He felt that on account of the children, and altogether, he had been playing it a bit low down.

He was not incapable, either, of appreciating Edith's attitude. She had never cross-questioned him, never asked him for a single detail, never laboured the subject, nor driven the point home, nor condescended even to try to find out how far things had really gone. She hadn't even told him how she knew; he was ashamed to ask. And, after that promise of forgiveness, she never referred to it; there was never the slightest innuendo, teasing, reproach. Yes, by Jove! Edith was wonderful! And so Bruce meant to play the game too.

For several days he asked the porter at the club if there were any letters, receiving the usual reply, "None, sir."

The third day he received the following note, and took it to read with enjoyment of the secrecy combined with a sort of self-important shame. Until now the hadn't communicated with her:—

"DEAR MR. OTTLEY,—Of course you know I'm not returning to the children after the holidays, nor am I going with you to Westgate. I'm very unhappy, for I fear I have offended Mrs. Ottley. She has always been very kind to me till now; but I shall let the matter rest. Under the circumstances I suppose I shall not see you any more. May I ask that you should not call or write. I and mother are going to spend the summer at Bexhill with some friends. Our address will be Sandringham, Seaview Road, Bexhill, if you like to write just one line to say good-bye. I fear I have been rather to blame in seeing you without Mrs. Ottley's knowledge, but you know how one's feelings sometimes lead one to do what one knows one ought not to . . ."

"Sandringham, indeed! Some boarding house, I suppose," said Bruce to himself.

"What a lot of 'ones'! . . . Fine grammar for a governess."

". . . Wishing you every happiness (I *shall* miss the children!). Yours sincerely,

"MARGARET TOWNSEND.

"*P.S.*—I shall never forget how happy I was with you and Mrs. Ottley."

Bruce's expression as he read the last line was rather funny.

"She's a silly little fool, and I sha'n't answer," he reflected.

Re-reading the letter, he found it more unsatisfactory still, and destroyed it.

The thought of Miss Townsend bored him unutterably; and indeed he was incapable of caring for any woman (however feebly) for more than two or three weeks. He was particularly fickle, vague, and scrappy in his emotions. Edith was the only woman for whom even a little affection could last, and he would have long tired of her but for her exceptional character and the extraordinary trouble and tact she used with him. He didn't appreciate her fine shades, he was not in love with her, didn't value her as another man might have done. But he was always coming back to a certain steady, renewed feeling of tenderness for her.

With the curious blindness common to all married people (and indeed to any people who live together), clever Edith had been entirely taken in, in a certain sense; she had always felt (until the "Townsend case") half disdainfully but satisfactorily certain of Bruce's fidelity. She knew that he had little sham flirtations, but she had never imagined his going anywhere near an intrigue. She saw now that in that she had been duped, and that if he didn't do more it was not from loyalty to her. Still, she now felt convinced that it wouldn't occur again. She had treated him well; she had spared him in the matter. He was a little grateful, and she believed he would be straight now, though her opinion of him had rather gone down. Edith always felt that she must go to the very extreme of loyalty to anyone who was faithful to her; she valued fidelity so deeply, and now this feeling was naturally relaxed a little. She hadn't the slightest desire for revenge, but she felt she had a slightly freer hand. She didn't see why she should, for instance, deprive herself of the pleasure of seeing Aylmer; she had not told him anything about it.

That day at the club, Bruce in his depression had a chat with Goldthorpe, his golfing companion and sometime confidant. Over a cigarette and other refreshments, Bruce murmured how he had put an end to the little affair for the sake of his wife.

"Rather jolly little girl, she was."

"Oh yes," said Goldthorpe indifferently. He thought Edith very attractive, and would have liked to have the duty of consoling her.

"One of those girls that sort of *get round* you, and appeal to you—*you* know."

"Oh yes."

"Grey eyes—no, by Jove! I should call them hazel, with black lashes, no, not exactly black—brown. Nice, white teeth, slim figure—perhaps a bit too straight. Brownish hair with a tinge of gold in the sun."

"Oh yes."

"About twenty," continued Bruce dreamily. He knew that Miss Townsend was thirty-two, but suspected Goldthorpe of admiring flappers, and so, with a subconscious desire to impress him, rearranged the lady's age.

"About twenty—if that. Rather long, thin hands—the hands of a lady. Well, it's all over now."

"That's all right," said Goldthorpe. He seemed to have had enough of this retrospective inventory. He looked at his watch and found he had an appointment.

Bruce, thinking he seemed jealous, smiled to himself.

For a few days after what had passed there was a happy reaction in the house. Everyone was almost unnaturally sweet and polite and unselfish about trifles to everybody else. Edith was devoting herself to the children, and Bruce had less of her society than usual. She seemed to assume they were to be like brother and sister. He wouldn't at present raise the question; thinking she would soon get over such a rotten idea. Besides, a great many people had left town; and they were, themselves, in the rather unsettled state of intending to go away in a fortnight. Though happy at getting off so easily, Bruce was really missing the meetings and notes (rather than the girl).

Fortunately, Vincy now returned; he was looking sunburnt and happy. He had been having a good time. Yet he looked a little anxious occasionally, as if perplexed.

One day he told Edith that he had just had a rather serious quarrel with someone who was awfully cross, and carried on like anything and wouldn't give over.

"I guess who she is. What does she want you to do?"

"She wants me to do what all my relations are always bothering me to do," said Vincy, "only with a different person."

"What, to marry?"

"Yes."

"To marry her, I suppose? Shall you?"

"I'm afraid not," he said. "I don't think I quite can."

"Don't you think it would be rather unkind to her?"

Neither of them had mentioned Miss Argles' name. The fact that Vincy referred to it at all showed her that he had recovered from his infatuation.

"But do you think I'm treating the poor girl badly?"

"Vincy, even if you adored her it would end unhappily. As you don't, you would both be miserable from the first day. Be firm. Be nice and kind to her and tell her straight out, and come and stay with us in the country."

"Well, that was rather my idea. Oh, but, Edith, it's hard to hurt anyone."

"You know I saw her driving with Aylmer that day, and I thought he liked her. I found I was wrong."

"Yes. He doesn't. I wish I could get some nice person to—er—take her out. I mean, take her on."

"What sort of person? She's pretty in her way. I daresay she'll attract someone."

"What sort of person? Oh, I don't know. Some nice earl would please her, or one of those artist chaps you read of in the feuilletons—the sort of artist who, when he once gets a tiny little picture skied at the Academy, immediately has fortune, and titles and things, rolling in. A little picture called 'Eventide' or 'Cows by Moonlight,' or something of that sort, in those jolly stories means ten thousand pounds a year at once. Jolly, isn't it?"

"Yes, Vincy dear, but we're not living in a feuilleton. What's really going to be done? Will she be nasty?"

"No. But I'm afraid Aunt Jessie will abuse me something cruel." He thought a little while. "In fact she has."

"What does she say?"

"She says I'm no gentleman. She said I had no business to lead the poor girl on, in a manner of speaking, and walk out with her, and pay her marked attention, and then not propose marriage like a gentleman."

"Then you're rather unhappy just now, Vincy?"

"Well, I spoke to *her* frankly, and said I would like to go on being her friend, but I didn't mean to marry. And *she* said she'd never see me again unless I did."

"And what else?"

"That's about all, thanks very much," said Vincy.

Here Bruce came in.

"Edith," he said, "have you asked Aylmer to come and stay with us at Westgate?"

"Oh no. I think I'd rather not."

"Why on earth not? How absurd of you. It's a bit selfish, dear, if you'll excuse my saying so. It's all very well for you: you've got the children and Vincy to amuse you (you're coming, aren't you, Vincy?). What price me? I must have someone else who can go for walks and play golf, a real pal, and so forth. I need exercise, and intellectual sympathy. Aylmer didn't say he had anywhere else to go."

"He's going to take his boy, Freddie, away to some seaside place. He doesn't like staying with people."

"All right, then. I shall go and ask him to come and stay at the hotel, for at least a fortnight. I shall go and ask him now. You're inconsistent, Edith. At one moment you seem to like the man, but as soon as I want to make a pleasant arrangement you're off it. So like a woman, isn't it, Vincy?" He laughed.

"Isn't it?" answered Vincy.

"Well, look here, I'm going right down to Jermyn Street purposely to tell him. I'll be back to dinner; do stop, Vincy."

Bruce was even more anxious than he used to be always to have a third person present whenever possible.

He walked through the hot July streets with that feeling of flatness—of the want of a mild excitement apart from his own home. He saw Aylmer and persuaded him to come.

While he was there a rather pretty pale girl, with rough red hair, was announced. Aylmer introduced Miss Argles.

"I only came for a minute, to bring back those books, Mr. Ross," she said shyly. "I can't stop."

"Oh, thank you so much," said Aylmer. "Won't you have tea?"

"No, nothing. I *must* go at *once*. I only brought you in the books myself to show you they were safe."

She gave a slightly coquettish glance at Aylmer, a half-observant glance at Bruce, sighed heavily and went away. She was dressed in green serge, with a turned-down collar of black lace. She wore black suède gloves, a gold bangle and a smart and pretty hat, the hat Vincy pretended had been given to *him* by Cissie Cavanack, his entirely imaginary cousin, and which he'd really bought for her in Bond Street.

"Well, I'll be off then. I'll tell Edith you'll write for rooms. Look sharp about it, because they soon go at the best hotels."

"At any rate I'll bring Freddie down for a week," said Aylmer, "and then we'll see."

"Who is that girl?" asked Bruce, as he left.

"She's a young artist, and I lent her some books of old prints she wanted. She's not a particular friend of mine—I don't care for her much."

Bruce didn't hear the last words, for he was flying out of the door. Miss Argles was walking very slowly; he joined her.

"Pardon me," he said, raising his hat. "It's so very hot—am I going your way? Would you allow me to see you home?"

"Oh, you're very kind, I'm sure," she said sadly. "But I don't think—— I live at Ravenscourt Park."

Bruce thought there was plenty of time.

"Why how very curious! That's just where I was going," said he boldly.

He put up his stick. Instead of a taxi a hansom drove up. Bruce hailed it.

"Always like to give these chaps a turn when I can," he said. It would take longer.

"How kind-hearted you are," murmured the girl. "But I'd really rather not, thank you."

"Then how shall you get back?"

"Walk to the Tube."

"Oh no; it's far too hot. Let me drop you, as I'm going in your direction."

He gave her a rather fixed look of admiration, and smiled. She gave a slight look back and got into the cab.

"What ripping red hair," said Bruce to himself as he followed her.

*

Before the end of the drive, which for him was a sort of adventure, Mavis had promised to meet Bruce when she left her Art School next Tuesday at a certain tea-shop in Bond Street.

Bruce went home happy and in good spirits again. There was no earthly harm in being kind to a poor little girl like this. He might do a great deal of good. She seemed to admire him. She thought him so clever. Funny thing, there was no doubt he had the gift; women liked him, and there you are. Look at Miss Mooney at the Mitchells' the other day, why, she was ever so nice to him; went for him like one o'clock; but he gave her no encouragement. Edith was there. He wouldn't worry her, dear girl.

As he came towards home he smiled again. And Edith, dear Edith—she, too, must be frightfully keen on him, when one came to think about it, to forgive him so readily about Margaret Tow—— Oh, confound Miss Townsend. This girl was a picture, a sort of Rossetti, and she had had such trouble lately—terrible trouble. The man she had been devoted to for years had suddenly thrown her over, heartlessly. ... What a brute he must have been! She was going to tell him all about it on Tuesday. That man must have been a fiend! ...

"Holloa, Vincy! So glad you're still here. Let's have dinner, Edie."

CHAPTER XXIII

AT LADY EVERARD'S

LADY EVERARD was sitting in her favourite attitude at her writing-table, with her face turned to the door. She had once been photographed at her writing-table, with a curtain behind her, and her face turned to the door. The photograph had appeared in *The Queen, The Ladies' Field, The Sketch, The Tatler, The Bystander, Home Chat, Home Notes, The Woman at Home,* and *Our Stately Homes of England*. It was a favourite photograph of hers; she had taken a fancy to it, and therefore she always liked to be found in this position. The photo had been called: "Lady Everard at work in her Music-Room."

What she was supposed to be working at, heaven only knew; for she never wrote a line of anything, and even her social notes and invitation cards were always written by her secretary.

As soon as a visitor came in, she rose from the

suspiciously clean writing-table, put down the dry pen on a spotless blotter, went and sat in a large brocaded arm-chair in front of some palms, within view of the piano, and began to talk. The music-room was large, splendid and elaborately decorated. There was a frieze all round, representing variously coloured and somewhat shapeless creatures playing what were supposed to be musical instruments. One, in a short blue skirt, was blowing at something; another in pink drapery (who squinted) was strumming on a lyre; other figures were in white, with their mouths open like young birds preparing to be fed by older birds. They represented Harmony in all its forms. There were other attempts at the classical in the decoration of the room; but Lady Everard herself had reduced this idea to bathos by huge quantities of signed photographs in silver frames, by large waste-paper baskets, lined with blue satin and trimmed with pink rosettes, by fans which were pockets, stuffed cats which were paperweights, oranges which were pincushions, and other debris from those charitable and social bazaars of which she was a constant patroness. With her usual curious combination of weak volubility and decided laying-down of the law, she was preparing to hold forth to young La France (whom she expected), on the subject of Debussy, Edvina, Marcoux, the appalling singing of all his young friends, his own good looks, and other subjects of musical interest, when Mr. Cricker was announced.

She greeted him with less eagerness, if less patronage, than her other protégé, but graciously offered him tea and permitted a cigarette.

Lady Everard went in for being at once *grande dame* and Bohemian. She was truly good-natured and kind, except to rivals in her own sphere, but when jealous she was rather redoubtable.

"I'm pleased to see you, my dear Willie," she said; "all the more because I hear Mrs. Mitchell has taken Wednesdays now. Not *quite* a nice thing to do, I think; although, after all, I suppose we could hardly really clash. True, we *do* happen to know a few of the same people." (By that Lady Everard meant she had snatched as many of Mrs. Mitchell's friends away as she thought desirable.) "But as a general rule I suppose we're not really in the same set. But perhaps you're going on there afterwards?"

That had been Mr. Cricker's intention, but he denied it, with surprise and apparent pain at the suspicion.

She settled down more comfortably.

"Ah, well, Mrs. Mitchell is an extremely nice, hospitable woman, and her parties are, I know, considered *quite* amusing, but I do think—I really do—that her husband carries his practical jokes and things a *little* too far. It isn't good form, it really isn't, to see a man of his age, with his face blacked, coming in after dinner with a banjo, calling himself the Musical White-eyed Kaffir, as he did the last time I was there. I find it *déplacé*—that's the word, *déplacé*. He seemed to think that we were all children at a juvenile party! I was saying so to Lord Rye only last night. Lord Rye likes it, I think, but he says Mr. Mitchell's mad—that's what it is, a little mad. Last time Lord Rye was there everybody had a present given them hidden in their table napkins. There had been some mistake in the parcels, I believe, and Miss Mooney—you know, the actress, Myra Mooney—received a safety razor, and Lord Rye a vanity bag. Everybody screamed with laughter, but I must say it seemed to me rather silly. I wasn't there myself."

"I was," said Mr. Cricker. "I got a very pretty little feather fan. I suppose the things really had been mixed up, and after all I was very glad of the fan; I was able to give it to——" He stopped, sighed and looked down on the floor.

"And is that affair still going on, Willie dear? It seems to me *such* a pity. I *do* wish you would try and give it up."

"I know, but she *won't*," he said, in a voice hoarse with anxiety. "Dear Lady Everard, you're a woman of the world, and know everything——"

She smiled. "Not everything, Willie; a little of music, perhaps. I know a good voice when I hear it. I have a certain *flair* for what's going to be a success in that direction, and of course I've been everywhere and seen everything. I've a certain natural knowledge of life, too, and keep well up to date with everything that's going on I knew about the Hendon Divorce Case long before anyone else, though it never came off after all, but that's not the point. But then I'm so discreet; people tell me things. At any rate, I always *know*."

Indeed, Lady Everard firmly believed herself to be a great authority on most subjects, but especially on contemporary gossip. This was a delusion. In reality she had that marvellous talent for not knowing things, that gift for ignorance, and genius for inaccuracy so frequently seen in that cultured section of society of which she was so popular and distinguished a member. It is a talent that rarely fails to please, particularly in a case like her own.

There is always a certain satisfaction in knowing that a woman of position and wealth, who plumes herself on her early knowledge and special information, is absolutely and entirely devoid of the one and incorrect in the other. A marked ignorance in a professionally well-informed person has always something touching and appealing to those who are able, if not willing, to set that person right. It was taken for granted among her acquaintances, and probably was one of the qualities that endeared her to them most, that dear Lady Everard was generally positive and always wrong.

"Yes, I do know most things, perhaps," she said complacently. "And one thing I know is that this woman friend of yours is making you perfectly miserable. You're longing to shake it off. Ah, I know you! You've far more real happiness in going to the opera with me than even in seeing her, and the more she pursues you the less you like it. Am I not right?"

"Yes, I suppose so. But as a matter of fact, Lady Everard, if she didn't—well—what you might call make a dash for it, I shouldn't worry about her at all."

"Men," continued Lady Everard, not listening, "only like coldness; coldness, reserve.

The only way in the world to draw a man on is to be always out to him, or to go away, and never even let him hear your name mentioned."

"I daresay there's a lot in that," said Cricker, wondering why she did not try that plan with young La France.

"Women of the present day," she continued, growing animated, "make such a terrible, terrible mistake! What do they do when they like a young man? Oh, I know! They write to him at his club; they call at his rooms and leave messages; they telephone whenever they can. The more he doesn't answer their invitations the more they invite him. It's appalling! And what's the result? Men are becoming cooler and cooler—as a class, I mean. Of course, there are exceptions. But it's such a mistake of women to run after the few young men there are. There are such a tremendous lot of girls and married women nowadays, there are so many more of them".

"Well, perhaps that's why they do it," said Cricker rather stupidly. "At any rate—oh, well, I know if my friend hadn't been so jolly nice to me at first and kept it up so—oh, well, you know what I mean—kept on keeping on, if I may use the expression, I should have drifted away from her ages ago. Because, you see, supposing I'm beginning so think about something else, or somebody else, she doesn't stand it; she won't stand it. And the awkward part is, you see, her being *on* the stage *and* married makes the whole thing about as awkward as a case of that sort can possibly be."

"I would not ask you her name for the world," said Lady Everard smoothly. "Of course I know she's a beautiful young comedy actress, or is it tragedy? I wonder if I could guess her first name? Will you tell me if I guess right?" She looked arch.

"Oh, I say, I can't tell you who it is, Lady Everard; really not."

"Only the first name? I don't *want* you to tell me; I'm discretion itself, I prefer not to know. The Christian name is not Margaretta, is it? Ah! no, I thought not. It's Irene Pettifer! There, I've guessed. The fact is, I always knew it, my dear boy. Your secret is safe with me. I'm the tomb! I——"

"Excuse me, Lady Everard," said Cricker, with every sign of annoyance, "it's no more Irene Pettifer than it's you yourself. Please believe me. First of all I don't *know* Irene Pettifer; I've never even seen her photograph —she's not young, not married, and an entirely different sort of person."

"What did I tell you? I knew it wasn't; I only said that to draw you. However, have a little more tea, or some iced coffee, it's so much more refreshing I always think. My dear Willie, I was only chaffing you. I knew perfectly well it wasn't either of the people I suggested. The point is, it seems to prey on your mind, and worry you, and you won't break it off."

"But how can I?"

"I will dictate you a letter," she said. "Far be it from me to interfere, and I don't pretend to know more about this sort of thing than anybody else. At the same time, if you'll take it down just as I tell it, and send it off, you'll find it will do admirably. Have you got a pencil?"

As if dully hypnotised, he took out a pencil and notebook.

"It would be awfully kind of you, Lady Everard. It might give me an idea anyway."

"All right."

She leant back and half closed her eyes, as if in thought; then started up with one finger out.

"We must be quick, because I'm expecting someone presently," she said. "But we've got time for this. Now begin. July 7th, 1912. Have you got that?"

"Yes, I've got that."

"Or, perhaps, just Thursday. Thursday looks

more casual, more full of feeling than the exact date. Got Thursday?"

"Yes, but it isn't Thursday, it's Friday."

"All right, Friday, or any day you like. The day is not the point. You can send it to-morrow, or any time you like. Wednesday. My dearest Irene."

"Her name's not Irene."

"Oh no, I forgot. Take that out. Dear Margaretta. Circumstances have occurred since I last had the pleasure of seeing you that make it absolutely impossible that I could ever meet you again."

"Oh, I say!"

"Go on. Ever see you or meet you again. You wish to be kind to her, I suppose?"

"Oh yes."

"Then say: Duty has to come between us, but God knows I wish you well." Tears were beginning to come to Lady Everard's eyes, and she spoke with a break in her voice. "I wish you well, Irene."

"It's not Irene."

"I wish you well, Margaretta. Some day in the far distant future you'll think of me, and be thankful for what I have done. It's for your good and my own happiness that we part now, and for ever. Adieu, and may God bless you. How do you sign yourself?"

"Oh, Willie."

"Very well then, be more serious this time: Always your faithful friend, William Stacey Cricker."

He glanced over the note, his face falling more and more, while Lady Everard looked more and more satisfied.

"Copy that out, word for word, the moment you go back, and send it off," she said, "and all the worst of your troubles will be over."

"I should think the worst is yet to come," said he ruefully.

"But you promise to do it, Willie? Oh, promise me?"

"Oh yes rather," said he half-heartedly.

"Word for word?"

"O Lord, yes. That's to say, unless anything——"

"Not a word, Willie; it will be your salvation. Come and see me soon, and tell me the result. Ah! here you are, cher maître!"

With a bright smile she welcomed Mr. La France, who was now announced, gently dismissing Willie with a push of the left hand.

"Good heavens!" he said to himself, as he got into the cab, "why, if I were to send a thing like that there would be murder and suicide! She'd show it to her husband, and he'd come round and knock me into a cocked hat for it. Dear Lady Everard—she's a dear, but she doesn't know anything about anything."

He tore the pages out of his pocket-book, and called out to the cabman the address of the Mitchells.

"Ah, chère madame, que je suis fatigué!" exclaimed La France, as he threw himself back against the cushions.

His hair was long and smooth and fair, so fair that he had been spoken of by jealous singers as a peroxide blond. His eyes were greenish, and he had dark eyebrows and eyelashes. He was good-looking. His voice in speaking was harsh, but his manner soft and insidious. His talents were cosmopolitan; his tastes international; he had no duties, few pleasures and that entire want of leisure known only to those who have practically nothing whatever to do.

"Fatigued? That's what you always say," said Lady Everard, laughing.

"But it is always true," he said, with a strong French accent.

"You should take more exercise, Paul. Go out more in the air. You lead too secluded a life."

"What exercises? I practise my voice every day, twenty minutes."

"Ah, but I didn't mean that. I mean in the open air—sport—that sort of thing."

"Ah, you wish I go horseback riding. Ver' nice, but not for me. I have never did it. I cannot begun now, Lady Everard. I spoil all the *velouté* of my voice. Have you seen again that pretty little lady I met here before? Delicious light brown hair, pretty blue eyes, a wonderful blue, a blue that seem to say to everyone something different."

"What!" exclaimed Lady Everard. "Are you referring to Mrs. Ottley?" She calmed down again. "Oh yes, she's charming, awfully sweet—devoted to her husband, you know—absolutely devoted to her husband; so rare and delightful nowadays in London."

"Oh yes, ver' nice. Me, I am devoted to 'er husband too. I go to see him. He ask me."

"What, without *me?*" exclaimed Lady Everard.

"I meet him the other night. He ask me to come round and sing him a song. I cannot ask if I may bring Lady Everard in my pocket."

"Really, Paul, I don't think that quite a nice joke to make, I must say." Then relenting she said: "I know it's only your artistic fun."

"So she ver' devoted to him? He have

great confidence in her; he trust her quite; he sure she never have any flirt?"

"He has every confidence; he's certain, absolutely certain!" exclaimed Lady Everard.

"He wait till she come and tell him, I suppose. 'E is right."

He continued in this strain for some time, constantly going back to his admiration for Edith, and then began (with a good deal of bitterness) on the subject of another young singer, whom he declared to be *un garçon charmant*, but no good. "He could not sing for nuts."

She heartily agreed, and they began to get on beautifully again, when she suddenly said to him:

"Is it true you were seen talking in the park to that girl Miss Turnbull, on Sunday?"

"If you say I was seen, I was. You could not know I talk to her unless I was seen. You could not know by wireless."

"Don't talk nonsense, Paul," she answered sharply. "The point isn't that you were seen, but that you did it."

"Who did it? Me? I didn't do anything."

"I don't think it's fair to me, I must say; it hurt my feelings that you should meet Amy Turnbull in the park and talk to her."

"But what could I say? It is ver' difficul.

I walk through the park; she walk through it with another lady. She speak to me. She say: Ah, dear Mr. La France, what pleasure to see you! I ask you, Lady Everard, could I, a foreigner, not even naturalised here, could I order her out of the park? Could I scream out to her: Go out, do not walk in ze Hyde Park! Lady Everard do not like you! I have no authority to say that. I am not responsible for the persons that walk in their own park in their own country. She might answer me to go to the devil! She might say to me: What, Lady Everard not like me, so I am not allowed in the park? What that got to do with it? In a case like this, chère madame, I have no legal power."

She laughed forgivingly and said:

"Ah, well, one mustn't be *too* exacting!" and as she showed some signs of a desire to pat his hair he rose, sat down to the piano, greatly to her disappointment, and filled up the rest of the time by improvising (from memory). It was a little fatiguing, as she thought it her duty to keep up an expression of acute rapture during the whole of the performance, which lasted at least three-quarters of an hour.

CHAPTER XXIV

MISS BENNETT

SINCE his return Aylmer saw everything through what he called a rose-coloured microscope—that is to say, every detail of his life, and everything connected with it, seemed to him perfect. He saw Edith as much as ever, and far less formally than before. She treated him with affectionate ease. She had admitted by her behaviour on the night he returned that she cared for him, and, for the moment, that was enough. A sort of general relaxation of formality, due to the waning of the season, and to people being too busy to bother, or already in thought away, seemed to give a greater freedom. Everyone seemed more natural, and more satisfied to follow their own inclinations and let other people follow theirs. London was getting stale and tired, and the last feverish flickers of the exhausted season alternated with a kind of languor in which nobody bothered much about anybody else's affairs. General interest was exhausted, and only a strong sense of self-preservation seemed to be left; people clung desperately to their last hopes. Edith was curiously peaceful and contented. She would have had scarcely any leisure but that her mother-in-law sometimes relieved her of the care of the children.

Being very anxious that they should not lose anything from Miss Townsend's absence, she gave them lessons every day.

One day, at the end of a history lesson, Archie said:

"Where's Miss Townsend?"

"She's at Bexhill."

"Why is she at Bexhill?"

"Because she likes it."

"Where's Bexhill?"

"In England."

"Why isn't Miss Townsend?"

"What do you mean, Archie?"

"Well, why isn't she Miss Townsend any more?"

"She is."

"But she's not our Miss Townsend any more. Why isn't she?"

"She's gone away."

"Isn't she coming back?"

"No."

Watching his mother's face he realised that she didn't regret this, so he said:

"Is Miss Townsend teaching anybody else?"

"I daresay she is, or she will, perhaps."

"What are their names?"

"How should I know?"

"Do you think she'll teach anybody else called Archie?"

"It's possible."

"I wonder if she'll ever be cross with the next boy she teaches."

"Miss Townsend was very kind to you," said Edith. "But you need not think about her any more, because you will be going to school when you come back from the holidays."

"That's what I told Dilly," said Archie. "But Dilly's not going to school. Dilly doesn't mind; she says she likes you better than Miss Townsend."

"Very kind of her, I'm sure," laughed Edith.

"You see you're not a real governess," said Archie, putting his arm round her neck. "You're not angry, are you, mother? Because you're not a real one it's more fun for us."

"How do you mean, I'm not a real governess?"

"Well, I mean we're not *obliged* to do what you tell us!"

"Oh, aren't you? You've got to; you're to go now because I expect Miss Bennett."

"Can't I see Miss Bennett?"

"Why do you want to see her?"

"I don't want to see her; but she always brings parcels. I like to see the parcels."

"They are not for you; she brings parcels because I ask her to do shopping for me. It's very kind of her."

She waited a minute, then he said:

"Mother, do let me be here when Miss Bennett brings the parcels. I'll be very useful. I can untie parcels with my teeth, like this. Look! I throw myself on the parcel just like a dog, and shake it and shake it and shake it, and then I untie it with my teeth. It would be awfully useful."

She refused the kind offer.

Miss Bennett arrived as usual with the parcels, looking pleasantly business-like and important.

"I wonder if these things will do?" she said, as she put them out on the table.

"Oh, they're sure to do," said Edith; "they're perfect."

"My dear, wait till you see them. I don't think I've completed all your list." She took out a piece of paper.

"Where did you get everything?" Edith asked, without much interest.

"At Boots', principally. Then the novels—Arnold Bennett, Maxwell—— Oh, and I've got you the poem: 'What is it?' by Gilbert Frankau."

"No, you mean, 'One of Us,'" corrected Edith.

"Then white serge for nurse to make Dilly's skirts—skirts a quarter of a yard long!—how sweet!—and heaps and heaps of muslin, you see, for her summer dresses. Won't she look an angel? Oh, and you told me to get some things to keep Archie quiet in the train." She produced a drum, a trumpet, and a mechanical railway train. "Will that do?"

"Beautifully."

"And here's your travelling cloak from the other place."

"It looks lovely," said Edith.

"Aren't you going to try it on?"

"No; it's sure to be all right."

"I never saw such a woman as you! Here are the hats. You've *got* to choose these."

Here Edith showed more interest. She put them on, said all the colour must be taken out of them, white put in one, black velvet in the other. Otherwise they would do.

"Thanks, Grace; you're awfully kind and

clever. Now do you know what you're going to do? You're going to the Academy with me and Aylmer. He's coming to fetch us."

"Oh, really—what fun!"

At this moment he arrived. Edith introduced them.

"I've been having such a morning's shopping," she said. "I deserve a little treat afterwards, don't I?"

"What sort of shopping? I'll tell you what you ought to have—a great cricket match when the shopping season's over, between the Old Selfridgians, and the Old Harrodians," he said, laughing.

They walked through acres of oil paintings and dozens of portraits of Chief Justices.

"I can't imagine anyone but Royalty enjoying these pictures," said Edith.

"They don't go to see pictures; they go to view exhibits," Aylmer answered.

Declaring they had "Academy headache" before they had been through the second room, they sat down and watched the people.

One sees people there that are to be seen nowhere else. An extraordinarily large number of clergymen, a peculiar kind of provincial, and strange Londoners, almost impossible to place, in surprising clothes.

Then they gave it up, and Aylmer took them out to lunch at a club almost as huge and noisy and as miscellaneous as the Academy itself. However, they thoroughly enjoyed themselves.

Edith and Bruce were to take up their abode in their little country house at Westgate next day.

CHAPTER XXV

AT WESTGATE

"I'VE got to go up to town on special business," said Bruce, one afternoon, after receiving a telegram which he had rather ostentatiously left about, hoping he would be questioned on the subject. It had, however, been persistently disregarded.
"Oh, have you?"
"Yes. Look at this wire."
He read aloud:
"*Wish to see you at once if possible come up to-day* M."
"Who *is* 'M'?"
"Mitchell, of course. Who should it be?" He spoke aggressively, then softened down to explanation, "Mitchell's in town a few days on business, too. I may be detained till Tuesday—or even Wednesday next."

Bruce had been to town so often lately, his manner was so vague, he seemed at once so happy and so preoccupied, so excited, so pleased, so worried, and yet so unnaturally good-tempered, that Edith had begun to suspect he was seeing Miss Townsend again.

The suspicion hurt her, for he had given his word of honour, and had been nice to her ever since, and amiable (though rather absent and bored) with the children.

She walked down to the station with him, though he wished to go in the cab which took his box and suit-case, but he did not resist her wish. On the way he said, looking round as if he had only just arrived and had never seen it before:

"This is a very nice little place. It's just the right place for you and the children. If I were you, I should stay on here."

It struck her he spoke in a very detached way, and some odd foreshadowing came to her.

"Why—aren't you coming back?" she asked jokingly.

"Me? *What* an idea! Yes, of course. But I've told you—this business of mine—well, it'll take a little time to arrange. Still, I expect to be back on Tuesday. Or quite on Wednesday— or sooner."

They walked on and had nearly reached the station.

"How funny you are, Bruce!"

"What do you mean? Are you angry with me for going up to see about important business? Why, here you've got Aylmer and his boy at the hotel, my mother and Vincy to stay with you. You've got plenty of companions. I don't suppose you'll miss me much. You see—a—this is a sort of business matter women don't understand. Women are incapable of understanding it."

"Of what nature is it?"

"How do you mean, nature? It's not of any particular *nature*. Nature, indeed! How like a woman! It's just business." He waited a minute. "Stockbroking; that's what it is. Yes, it's stockbroking. I want to see a chap who's put me in to a good thing. A perfectly safe thing. No gambling. But one has to see into it, you see. Mitchell wants to see me at once, you see. Do you see? You saw his wire, didn't you? I've explained, haven't I? Aren't you satisfied with my explanation?"

"*You* appear to be—very. But I'm not asking you to tell me any details about the business, whatever it may be."

They arrived at the station, and Bruce gave her what she thought a very queer look. It was a mixture of fear, daring, caution and a sort of bravado. Anxiety was in it, as well as a pleased self-consciousness.

"Tell me, frankly, something I'd like to know, Bruce."

"Are you getting suspicious of me, Edith? That's not like you. Mind you, it's a great mistake in a woman; women should always trust. Mistrust sometimes drives a man to—to—— Oh, anyhow it's a great mistake."

"I only want you to tell me something, Bruce. I'll believe you implicitly if you'll answer. . . . Do you ever see Miss Townsend now?"

"Never, on my honour! I swear it." He spoke with such genuine good faith that she believed him at once.

"Thanks. I'm glad. And—have you never since——"

"Never seen her, never written to her, never communicated with her since she left! Don't know where she is and don't care. Now you do believe me?" he asked, with all the earnestness and energy of truth.

"Absolutely. Forgive me for asking."

"Oh, that's all right."

He was relieved, and smiled.

"All right, Bruce dear. I'm glad. It would have worried me."

"Now go, Edith. Don't bother to wait till I get in. I'll write to you—I'll write to you soon."

She still lingered, seeing something odd in his manner.

"Give my love to my mother," he said, looking away. "I say—Edith."

"Yes, dear?"

"Oh, nothing."

She waited on till the train started. His manner was alternately peevish and kind, but altogether odd. Her last glimpse was a rather pale smile from Bruce as he waved his hand and then turned to his paper. . . .

"Well, what *does* it matter so long as he *has* gone!" exclaimed Aylmer impatiently, when she expressed her wonder at Bruce's going. The tide was low, and they went for a long walk over the hard shining sand, followed by Archie picking up wonderful shells and slipping on the green seaweed. Everything seemed fresh, lovely. She herself was as fresh as the sea breeze, and Aylmer seemed to her as strong as the sea. (Privately, Edith thought him irresistible in country clothes.) Edith had everything here to make her happy, including Bruce's mother, who relieved her of the children when she wanted rest and in whose eyes she was perfection.

She saw restrained adoration in Aylmer's eyes, love and trust in the eyes of the children.

She had all she wanted. And yet—something tugged at her heart, and worried her. She had a strange and melancholy presentiment.

But she threw it off. Probably there was nothing really wrong with Bruce; perhaps only one of those little imaginary romances that he liked to fabricate for himself; or, perhaps, it was really business? It was all right if Mr. Mitchell knew about it. Yet she could not believe that "M" *was* Mitchell. Bruce had repeated it too often; and, why on earth should Mitchell suddenly take to sending Bruce fantastic telegrams and signing them, for no reason, with an initial? . . .

CHAPTER XXVI

GOGGLES

"WHAT divine heavenly pets and ducks of angels they are!" exclaimed Lady Everard rather distractedly. "Angels! Divine! And so good, too! I never saw such darlings in my life. Look at them, Paul. Aren't they sweet?"

Lady Everard with her party (what Aylmer called her performing troupe) had driven over to Westgate, from where she was staying in the neighbourhood, to have tea with Edith. She had brought with her a sort of juvenile party, consisting of Mr. Cricker, Captain Willis and, of course, Paul La France, the young singer. She never moved without him. She explained that two other women had been coming also, but they had deserted her at the last minute.

Paul La France had been trying for an hour and a half to make eyes through motor goggles, which, naturally, was not a success; so he seemed a little out of temper. Archie was staring at him as if fascinated. He went up and said:

"Voulez-vous lend me your goggles?"

"Mais certainement! Of course I will. Voilà mon petit."

"The darling! How sweet and amusing of him! But they're only to be used in the motor, you know. Don't break them, darling, will you? Monsieur will want them again. Ah! how sweet he looks!" as he put them on, "I never saw such a darling in the whole course of my life! Look at him, Mrs. Ottley. Look at him, Paul!"

"Charmant. C'est délicieux," grumbled La France.

"What a charming little lawn this is, going right down to the sea, too. Oh, Mr. Ross, is that you? Isn't this a delightful little house? More tea? Yes, please. Mr. La France doesn't take sugar, and——"

"You don't know what I am now," said Archie, having fixed the goggles on his own fair head, to the delight of Dilly.

"Oh, I guess what you are! You're a motorist, aren't you, darling? That's it! It's extraordinary how well I always get on with children, Mrs. Ottley," explained Lady Everard. "I daresay it's through being used to my little grandchildren, Eva's two angels, you know, but I never see them because I can't stand their noise, and yet I simply adore them. Pets!"

"What am I?" asked Archie, in his persistent way, as he walked round the group on the lawn, in goggles, followed closely by Dilly, saying, "Yes, what is he?" looking exactly like a live doll, with her golden hair and blue ribbons.

"You're a motorist, darling."

"No, I'm not a silly motorist. Guess what I am?"

"It's so difficult to guess, such hot weather! Can you guess, Paul?"

"I sink he is a nuisance," replied the Frenchman, laughing politely.

"No, that's wrong. You guess what I am."

"Guess what he is," echoed Dilly.

"O Lord! what does it matter? What I always say is—live and let live, and let it go at that," said Captain Willis, with his loud laugh. "What, Mrs. Ottley? But they won't do it, you know—they won't—and there it is!"

"Guess what I am," persisted Archie.

"Never mind what you are; do go and sit down, and take those things off," said Edith.

"Not till you guess what I am."

"Does Dilly know?"

"No, Dilly doesn't know. Guess what I am, grandmamma!"

"I give it up."

"I thought you'd never guess. Well, I'm a blue-faced mandrill!" declared Archie, as he took the goggles off reluctantly and gave them back to La France, who put them under his chair.

"Yes, he's a two-faced mangle," repeated Dilly.

He turned round on her sharply. "Now, don't talk nonsense! You're a silly girl. I never said anything about being a two-faced mangle; I'm a blue-faced mandrill."

"Well, I said so; a two-faced mangle."

"Don't say anything at all if you can't say it right," said Archie, raising his voice and losing his temper.

"Well, they's both the same."

"No, they jolly well aren't."

He drew her a little aside. "A blue-faced mandrill, silly, is *real*; it's in my natural history book."

"Sorry," said Dilly apologetically.

"In my natural history book it is, a *real* thing. I'm a blue-faced mandrill. . . . Now say it after me."

"You's a two-faced mangle."

"Now you're doing it on purpose! If you weren't a little girl, Dilly——"

"I wasn't doing it on purpose."

"Oh, get away before I hit you! You're a silly little fool."

She slowly walked away, calling out: "And you're a silly two-faced mangle," in a very irritating tone. Archie made a tremendous effort to ignore her, then he ran after her saying:

"Will you shut up or will you not?"

Aylmer seized hold of him.

"What are you going to do, Archie?"

"Teach Dilly what I am. She says—— Oh, she's *such* a fool!"

"No, Archie, leave her alone; she's only a baby. Come along, old boy. Give Mr. Cricker a cup of tea; he hasn't had one yet."

Archie was devoted to Aylmer. Following him, he handed the tea to Mr. Cricker, saying pathetically:

"I'm a blue-faced mandrill, and she knew it. I told her so. Aren't girls fools? They do worry!"

"They *are* torments," said Aylmer.

"I wish that Frenchman would give me his goggles to keep! He doesn't want them."

"I'll give you a pair," said Aylmer.

"Thanks," said Cricker, "I won't have any

tea. I wish you'd come and have a little talk with me, Ross. Can I have a word with you alone?"

Aylmer good-naturedly went aside with him.

"It's worse than ever," said Cricker, in low, mysterious tones. "Since I've been staying with Lady Everard it's been wire, wire, wire—ring, ring, ring—and letters by every post! You see, I thought it was rather a good plan to get away for a bit, but I'm afraid I shall have to go back. Fancy, she's threatened suicide, and telling her husband, and confiding in Lady Everard! And giving up the stage, and oh, goodness knows what! There's no doubt the poor child is absolutely raving about me. No doubt whatever."

Aylmer was as sympathetic as he knew how.

The party was just going off when La France found that the goggles had disappeared. A search-party was organised; great excitement prevailed; but in the end they went away without the glasses.

When Dilly had just gone to sleep in her cot a frightening figure crept into her room and turned on the electric light.

"Oh, Archie! *What* is it! Who is it! Oh! . . . Oh!"

"Don't be frightened," said Archie, in his

deepest voice, obviously hoping she would be frightened. He was in pyjamas and goggles. "Don't be frightened! *Now! Say what I am. What am I?*"

"A blue-faced mandrill," she whined.

He took off the goggles and kissed her.

"Right! Good-night, old girl!"

CHAPTER XXVII

THE ELOPEMENT

THE following Tuesday, Edith, Aylmer, Vincy and Mrs. Ottley were sitting on the verandah after dinner. They had a charming little verandah which led on to a lawn, and from there straight down to the sea. It was their custom to sit there in the evening and talk. The elder Mrs. Ottley enjoyed these evenings, and the most modern conversation never seemed to startle her. She would listen impassively, or with a smile, as if in silent approval, to the most monstrous of paradoxes or the most childish chaff.

Aylmer's attention and kind thought for her had absolutely won her heart. She consulted him about everything, and was only thoroughly satisfied when he was there. His strong, kind, decided voice, his good looks, his decision, and a sort of responsible impulsiveness, all appealed to her immensely. She looked up to him, in a kind of admiring maternal way; Edith often wondered, did she not see Aylmer's devotion? But, if she did, Mrs. Ottley thought nothing of it. Her opinion of Edith was so high that she trusted her in any complications. . . .

"Isn't Bruce coming down to-night?" she asked Edith.

"I'm to have a wire."

"Ah, here's the last post. Perhaps he's written instead."

Vincy fetched the letters. There was one from Bruce.

Edith went into the drawing-room to read it; there was not sufficient light on the verandah....

In growing amazement she read the following words:—

"DEAR EDITH,—I hope what I am about to tell you will not worry you too much. At any rate I do hope you will not allow it to affect your health. It is inevitable, and you must make up your mind to it as soon as possible. I say this in no spirit of unkindness; far from it. It is hard to me to break the news to you, but it must be done.

"Mavis Argles and I are all in all to each other. We have made up our minds on account of certain *circumstances* to throw in our lot together, and we are starting for Australia to-

THE ELOPEMENT

day. When this reaches you, we shall have started. I enclose the address to write to me.

"In taking this step I have, I am sure, acted for the best. It may cause you great surprise and pain. I regret it, but we met and became very quickly devoted to one another. She cannot live without me. What I am doing is my duty. I now ask you, and believe you will grant my request, to make arrangements to *give me my freedom as soon as possible*. Mind you do this, Edith, for it is really my duty to give my name to Mavis, who, as I have said, is devoted to me heart and soul, and cannot live without me.

"I shall always have the greatest regard and respect for you, and *wish you well*.

"I am sorry also about my mother, but you must try and explain that it is for the best. You also will know exactly what to do, and how to bring up the children just as well without me as with.

"Hoping this sudden news will not affect your health in any way, and that you will try and stay on a good while at Westgate, as I am sure the air is doing you good, believe me, yours affectionately as always,

"BRUCE."

"*P.S.*—Mind you don't forget to divorce me as soon as you can for Mavis's sake. Vincy will give you all the advice you need. Don't think badly of me; I have meant well. Try and cheer up. I am sorry not to write more fully, but you can imagine how I was rushed to catch to-day's steamer."

She sat alone gazing at the letter under the light. She was divided at first between a desire to laugh and cry. Bruce had actually eloped! His silly weakness had culminated, his vanity had been got hold of. Vincy's horrid little art-student had positively led him into running away, and leaving his wife and children.

Controlling herself, Edith went to the verandah and said to Mrs. Ottley that Bruce wasn't coming back for a day or two, that she had neuralgia and was going to retire, but begged Aylmer not to go yet. Of course at this he went at once.

The next morning Aylmer at his hotel received a little note asking him to come round and see Edith, while the others were out.

It was there, in the cool, shady room, that Edith showed him the letter.

"Good God!" he exclaimed, looking simply wild with joy. "This is too marvellous!—too heavenly! Do you realise it? Edith, don't you see he wants you to make him free? You will be my wife—that's settled—that's fixed up."

He looked at her in delight almost too great for expression.

Edith knew she was going to have a hard task now. She was pale, but looked completely composed. She said:

"You're wrong, Aylmer. I'm not going to set him free."

"What?" he almost shouted. "Are you mad? What! Stick to him when he doesn't want you! Ruin the wretched girl's life!"

"That remains to be seen. I don't believe everything in the letter. The children——"

"Edith!" he exclaimed. "What—when he doesn't *want* the children—when he deserts them?"

"He is their father."

"Their father! Then, if you were married to a criminal who implored you to divorce him you wouldn't, because he was their father!"

"Bruce is not a criminal. He is not bad. He is a fool. He has behaved idiotically, and I can never care for him in the way I used to, but I mean to give him a chance. I'm not going to jump at his first real folly to get rid of him. . . . Poor Bruce!"

She laughed.

Aylmer threw himself down in an arm-chair, staring at her.

"You amaze me," he said. "You amaze me. You're not human. Do you adore this man, that you forgive him everything? You don't even seem angry."

"I don't adore him, that is why I'm not so very angry. I was terribly hurt about Miss Townsend. My pride, my trust were hurt, but after that I can't ever feel that personal jealousy any more. What I have got to think of is what is best."

"Edith, you don't care for me. I'd better go away." He turned away; he had tears in his eyes.

"Oh, don't, Aylmer! You know I do!"

"Well, then, it's all right. Fate seems to have arranged this on purpose for us—don't you know, dear, how I'd be good to the children? How I'd do anything on this earth for them? Why, I'd reconcile Mrs. Ottley to it in ten minutes; I'd do *anything!*" He started up.

"I'm not going to let Mrs. Ottley know anything about it for the present."

"You're not going to tell her?"

"No. I shall invent a story to account for his absence. No one need know. But, of course, if, later—I mean if he persists——"

"Oh, Edith, don't be a fool! You're throwing away our happiness when you've got it in your hand."

"There are some things that one *can't* do," said Edith. "It goes against the grain. I can't take advantage of his folly to make the path smoother—for myself. What will become of him when they quarrel! It's all nonsense. Bruce is only weak. He's a very good fellow, really. He has no spirit, and not much intellect; but with us to look after him," she unconsciously said us, and could not help smiling at the absurdity of it, "he will get along all right yet."

"Edith, you're beyond me," said Aylmer. "I give up understanding you."

She stood up again and looked out of the window.

"Let him have his silly holiday and his elopement and his trip! He thinks it will make a terrific sensation! And I hope she will be seasick. I'm sure she will; she's the sort of woman who would, and then—after——"

"And you'll take him back? You have no pride, Edith."

She turned round. "Take him back?—yes; officially. He has a right to live in his own house, with his own children. Why, ever since I found out about Miss Townsend . . . I'm sure I was nice to him, but only like a sister. Yes. I feel just like a sister to him now."

"Oh, good God! I haven't patience with all this hair-splitting nonsense. Brotherly husbands who run away with other girls, and beg you to divorce them; sisterly wives who forgive them and stick to them against their will. . . ."

He suddenly stopped, and held out his hand.

"Forgive me, Edith. I believe whatever you say is right. Will you forgive me?"

"You see, it's chiefly on account of the children. If it weren't for them I *would* take advantage of this to be happy with you. At least—no—I'm not sure that I would; not if I thought it would be Bruce's ruin."

"And you don't think I'd be good to the children?"

"Good? I know you would be an angel to them! But what's the use? I tell you I can't do it."

"I won't tease you, I won't worry you any more." he said, in a rather broken voice. "At any rate, think what a terrible blow this is to me. You show me the chance of heaven, then you voluntarily dash it away. Don't you think you ought to consult someone? You have asked no one?"

"I have consulted *you*," she said, with a slight smile.

"You take no notice of what I say."

"As a matter of fact, I don't wish to consult anyone. I have made my own decision. I have written my letter."

She took it out of her bag. It was directed to Bruce, at the address he had given her in Australia.

"I suppose you won't let me read it?" he said sadly.

"I think I'd rather not," she said.

Terribly hurt, he turned to the door.

"No—no, you shall read it!" she exclaimed. "But don't say anything, make no remark about it. You shall read it because I trust you, because I really care for you."

"Perhaps I oughtn't to," he said. "No, dear; keep it to yourself." His delicacy had revived and he was ashamed of his jealousy.

But now she insisted on showing it to him, and he read:

"DEAR BRUCE,—I'm not going to make any appeal to your feelings with regard to your mother and the children, because if you had thought even of me a little this would not have happened. I'm very, very sorry for it. I believe it happened from your weakness and foolishness, or you could not have behaved with such irresponsibility, but I'm trying to look at it quite calmly. I therefore propose to do nothing at all for three months. If I acted on your suggestion you might regret it ever after. If in three months you write to me again in the same strain, still desiring to be free, I will think of it, though I'm not sure that I should do it even then. But in case you change your mind I propose to tell nobody, not even your mother. By the time you get this letter, it will be six weeks since yours to me, and you may look at things differently. Perhaps by then you will be glad to hear that I have told your mother merely that you have been ordered away for a change, and I shall say the same to anyone else who inquires for you. If you feel after this time still responsible, and that you have a certain duty, still remember, even *so*, you might be very unhappy together all your lives. Excuse me, then, if I don't take you at your word.

"Another point occurs to me. In your hurry and excitement, perhaps you forgot that your father's legacy depended on the condition that you should not leave the Foreign Office before you were fifty. That is about fourteen years from now. If you are legally freed, and marry

Miss Argles, you could hardly go back there. I think it would be practically impossible under those circumstances, while if you live in Australia you will have hardly any means. I merely remind you of this, in case you had forgotten.

"I shall regard it all as an unfortunate aberration; and if you regret it, and change your mind, you will be free at any time you like to come back and nothing shall be ever said about it. But I'm not begging you to do so. I may be wrong; perhaps she's the woman to make you happy. Let me know within three months how you feel about it. No one will suffer except myself during this time, as I shall keep it from your mother, and shall remain here during this time. Perhaps you will be very angry with me that I don't wish to take you at your word, Bruce. At first I thought I would, but I'm doing what I think right, and one cannot do more.

"I'm not going to reproach you, for if you don't feel the claims of others on you, my words will make no difference.

"Think over what I say. Should you be unhappy and wish to separate from her without knowing how, and if it becomes a question of money, as so many things do, I would help you. I did not remind you about your father's legacy to induce you to come back. If you really find happiness in the way you expect, we could arrange it. You see, I have thought of everything, in one night. But you *won't* be happy.

"Edith Ottley."

"Remember, whenever you like to come back, you will be welcomed, and nothing shall ever be said about it."

Aylmer gave her back the letter. He was touched.

"You see," she said eagerly, "I haven't got a grain of jealousy. All that part is quite finished. That's the very reason why I can judge calmly."

She fastened up the letter, and then said with a smile:

"And now, let's be happy the rest of the summer. Won't you?"

He answered that she was *impayable*—marvellous—that he would help her—devote himself to doing whatever she wished. On consideration he saw that there was still hope.

CHAPTER XXVIII

BRUCE RETURNS

"NEVER, Edith!" exclaimed Vincy, fixing his eyeglass in his eye, and opening his mouth in astonishment. "Never! Well, I'm gormed!"

A week had passed since the news of Bruce's elopement. The little group at Westgate didn't seem to have much been affected by it; and this was the less surprising as Aylmer and Edith had kept it to themselves. Mrs. Ottley listened imperturbably to Edith's story, a somewhat incoherent concoction, but told with dash and decision, that Bruce had been ordered away for a sea-voyage for fear of a nervous breakdown. She cried a little, said nothing, kissed Edith more than usual, and took the children away for longer walks and drives. With a mother's flashlight of intuition she felt at once certain there was something wrong, but she didn't wish to probe the subject. Her confidence in Edith reached the point of superstition; she would never ask her questions. Edith had assured her that Bruce would come back all right, and that was enough. Personally, Mrs. Ottley much preferred the society of Aylmer to that of her son. Aylmer was far more amusing, far more considerate to her, and to everybody else, and he didn't use his natural charm for those who amused him only, as the ordinary fascinating man does. Probably there was at the back of his attentions to Mrs. Ottley a vague idea that he wanted to get her on his side—that she might be a useful ally; but he was always charming to elderly women, and inclined to be brusque with younger ones, excepting Edith; he remembered his own mother with so great a cult of devotion, and his late wife with such a depressed indifference.

Edith had asked Aylmer to try and forget what had happened—to make himself believe that Bruce had really only gone away medicinally. For the present, he did as she wished, but he was longing to begin talking to her on the subject again, both because it interested him passionately from the psychological point of view, and far more, naturally, because he had hopes of persuading her in time. She was not bound by letter; she could change her mind. Bruce might, and possibly would, insist.

There was difficulty in keeping the secret from Vincy, who was actually staying in the house, and whose wonderful nerves and whimsical mind were so sensitive to every variation of his surroundings. He had the gift of reading people's minds. But it never annoyed anyone; one felt he had no illusions; that he sympathised with one's weaknesses and follies and, in a sense, enjoyed them, from a literary point of view. Probably his friends forgave his clear vision for the sake of his interest. Most people would far rather be seen through than not be seen at all.

One day Vincy, alone on the beach with Edith, remarked that he wondered what had happened to Mavis.

Edith told him that she had run away with a married man.

"Never, Edith!" he exclaimed. "Who would have thought it! It seems almost too good to be true!"

"Don't say that, Vincy."

"But how did you hear it? You know everything."

"I heard it on good authority. I *know* it's true."

"And to think I was passing the remark only the other day that I thought I ought to look her up, in a manner of speaking, or write, or something," continued Vincy; "and who *is* the poor dear man? Do you know?"

He looked at her with a sudden vague suspicion of he knew not what.

"Bruce was always inclined to be romantic, you know," she said steadily.

"Oh, give over!"

"Yes, that's it; I didn't want anyone to know about it. I'm so afraid of making Mrs. Ottley unhappy."

"But you're not serious, Edith?"

"I suppose I'd better show you his letter. He tells me to ask your advice."

She gave it to him.

"There is only one word for what I feel about it," Vincy said, as he gave it back. "I'm gormed! Simply gormed! Gormed, Edith dear, is really the only word."

"I'm not jealous," said Edith. "My last trouble with Bruce seems to have cured me of any feeling of the kind. But I have a sort of pity and affection for him still in a way—almost like a mother! I'm really afraid he will be miserable with her, and then he'll feel tied to her and be wretched all his life. So I'm giving him a chance."

He looked at her with admiring sympathy.

"But what about other friends?"

"Well—oh, you know——"

"Edith, I'm awfully sorry; I wish I'd married her now, then she wouldn't have bothered about Bruce."

"But you can't stand her, Vincy."

"I know, Edith dear; but I'd marry any number of people to prevent anything tiresome for you. And Aylmer, of course—Edith, really, I think Aylmer ought to go away; I'm sure he ought. It is a mistake to let him stay here under these circumstances."

"Why?" said Edith. "I don't see that; if I were going to take Bruce at his word, then it would be different, of course."

"It does seem a pity not to, in some ways; everything would be all nicely settled up, just like the fourth act of a play. And *then* I should be glad I hadn't married Mavis. . . . Oh, do let it be like the fourth act, Edith."

"How can life be like a play? It's hopeless to attempt it," she said rather sadly.

"Edith, do you think if Bruce knew—how much you liked Aylmer—he would have written that letter?"

"No. And I don't believe he would ever have gone away."

"Still, I think you ought to send Aylmer away now."

"Why?" she repeated. "Nothing could be more intensely correct. Mrs. Ottley's staying with me—why shouldn't I have the pleasure of seeing Aylmer because Bruce is having a heavenly time on board ship?"

"I suppose there's that point of view," said Vincy, rather bewildered. "I say, Edith!"

"Yes?"

"About Bruce having a heavenly time on board ship—a—she always grumbles; she's always complaining. She's never, never satisfied. . . . She keeps on making scenes."

"So does Bruce."

"Yes. But I suppose if there's a certain predicament—then—— Oh, Edith—are you unhappy?"

"No, not a bit now. I think I'm only really unhappy when I'm undecided. Once I've taken a line—no matter what it is—I can be happy again. I can adjust myself to my good fortune."

Curiously, when Edith had once got over the pain and shock that the letter first gave her, she was positively happier now than she ever had been before. Bruce really must have been a more formidable bore than she had known, since his absence left such a delicious freedom. The certainty of having done the right, the wisest thing, was a support, a proud satisfaction.

During these summer days Aylmer was not so peacefully happy. His devotion was assiduous, silent, discreet, and sometimes his feelings were almost uncontrollable, but he hoped; and he consoled himself by the thought that some day he would really have his wish—anything might happen; the chances were all in his favour.

What an extraordinary woman she was—and how pretty—how subtle; how perfect their life might be together. . . .

He implored Vincy to use his influence.

"I can't see Edith in anything so crude as the—as—that court," Vincy said.

"But Bruce begs her to do it. What could their life be together afterwards? It's simply a deliberate sacrifice."

"There's every hope that Miss Argles will never let him go," said Vincy. "One has to be very firm to get away from her. Oh, ever so firm, and *obstinate*, you can't think! How many times a day she must be reproaching Bruce—that will be rather a change for him. However, anything may happen," said Vincy soothingly. He still maintained, for he had a very strong sense of propriety in matters of form, that Aylmer ought to go away. But Edith would not agree.

So the children played and enjoyed themselves, and sometimes asked after their father, and Mrs. Ottley, though a little anxious, enjoyed herself too, and Edith had never been so happy. She was having a holiday. She dismissed all trouble and lived in a sort of dream.

Towards the end of the summer, hearing no more from Bruce, Aylmer grew still more hopeful; he began to regard it as practically settled. The next letter in answer to Edith's would doubtless convince her, and he would then persuade her; it was, tacitly, he thought, almost agreed now; it was not spoken of between them, but he believed it was all right. . . .

Aylmer had come back to London in the early days of September and was wandering through his house thinking how he would have it done up and how he wouldn't leave it when they were married, when a telephone message summoned him to Knightsbridge.

He went, and found the elder Mrs. Ottley just going away. He thought she looked at him rather strangely.

"I think Edith wants to speak to you," she said, as she left the room. "Dear Edith! Be nice to her." And she fled.

Aylmer waited alone, looking round the

room that he loved because he associated it with her.

It was one of the first cold damp days of the autumn, and there was a fire. Edith came in, in a dark dress, looking pale, and different, he thought. She had seemed the very spirit of summer only a day or two before.

A chill presentiment struck to his heart.

"You've had a letter? Go on; don't keep me in suspense." He spoke with nervous impatience, and no self-restraint.

She sat down by him. She had no wish to create an effect, but she found it difficult to speak.

"Yes, I've had a letter," she said quietly. "They've quarrelled. They quarrelled on board. He hates her. He says he would rather die than remain with her. He's written me a rather nice letter. They quarrelled so frightfully that a young man on board interfered," she said, smiling faintly. "As soon as they arrived the young man married her. He's a commercial traveller. He's only twenty-five. . . . It seems he pitied her so much that he proposed to her on board, and she left Bruce. It wasn't true about the predicament. It was—a mistake. Bruce was grateful for my letter. He's glad I've not told anyone—not done anything. Now the children will never know. But I've told Mrs. Ottley all about it. I thought I'd better, now it's over. She won't ask him questions. . . . Bruce is on his way home."

"All right!" said Aylmer, getting up. "Let him come. Forgive him again, that's right! Would you have done that for *me*?"

"No! Never! If you had once been unfaithful, and I knew it, I'd never have forgiven you."

"I quite believe it. But why?"

"Because I care for you too much. If you had been in Bruce's position I should never have seen you again. With him it's different. It's a feeling of—it's for him, not for me. I've felt no jealousy, no passion, so I could judge calmly."

"All right," repeated Aylmer ironically; "all right! Judge calmly! Do the right thing. You know best." He stopped a moment, and then said, taking his hat: "I understand now. I see clearly at last. You've had the opportunity and you wouldn't take it; you don't care for me. I'm going."

He went to the door.

"Oh, come back, Aylmer! Don't go like that! You know I care for you, but what could I do? I foresaw this. . . . You know, I can't feel *no* responsibility about Bruce. I couldn't make my happiness out of someone else's misery. He would have been miserable and, not only that, it would have been his ruin. Bruce could never be safe, happy, or all right, except here."

"And you think he'll alter, now, be grateful and devoted, I suppose—appreciate you?"

"Do people alter?" she answered.

"I neither know nor care if he will, but you? *I* could have made you happy. You won't let me. Oh, Edith, how could you torture me like this all the summer?"

"I didn't mean to torture you. We enjoyed being together."

"Yes. But it makes this so much harder."

"It would be such a risk!" she answered.

"But is anything worth having unless you're ready to risk everything to get it?"

"I *would* risk everything, for myself. But not for others. . . . If you feel you want to go away," she said, "let it be only for a little while."

"A little while! I hope I shall *never* see you again! Do you think I'm such a miserable fool—do you think I could endure the position of a tame cat? You forget I'm a man! . . . No; I'll never see you again now, not if it kills me!"

At these words, the first harsh ones she had ever heard from him, her nerves gave way, and she burst into tears.

This made him irresolute, for his tenderheartedness almost reached the point of weakness. He went up to her, as she lifted her head, and looked at her once more. Then he said:

"No, you've chosen. You *have* been cruel to me, and you're too good to him. But I suppose you must carry out your own nature, Edith. I've been the victim. That's all."

"And won't you be friends?" she said.

"No. I won't and I can't."

He waited one moment more.

"If you'll change your mind—you still can—we can still be happy. We can be everything to each other. . . . Give him up. Give him up."

"I can't," said Edith.

"Then, good-bye."

CHAPTER XXIX

INTELLECTUAL SYMPATHY

"WHAT are you going to wear to-night, Edith?"

"Oh; anything!"

"Don't say anything. I don't wish you to wear anything. I'm anxious you should look your best, really nice, especially as we haven't been to the Mitchells' for so long. Wear your new blue dress."

"Very well."

Bruce got up and walked across the room and looked in the glass.

"Certainly, I'm a bit sunburnt," he remarked thoughtfully. "But it doesn't suit me badly, not really badly; does it?"

"Not at all."

"Edith."

"Yes?"

"If I've spoken about it once, I've spoken about it forty times. This ink-bottle is too full."

"I'll see about it."

"Don't let me have to speak about it again, will you? I wonder who will be at the Mitchells' to-night?"

"Oh, I suppose there'll be the new person—the woman with the dramatic contralto foghorn voice; and the usual people: Mr. Cricker, Lady Everard, Miss Mooney——"

"Miss Mooney! I hope not! I can't stand that woman. I think she's absurd; she's a mass of affectation and prudishness. And—Edith!"

"Yes?"

"I don't want to interfere between mother and daughter—I know you're perfectly capable and thoroughly well suited to bringing up a girl, but I really do think you're encouraging Dilly in too great extravagance."

"Oh! In what way?"

"I found her making a pinafore for her doll out of a lace flounce of real old Venetian lace. Dilly said she found it on the floor. 'On the floor, indeed,' I said to her. 'You mustn't use real lace!' She said, 'Why not? It's a real doll!' Lately Dilly's got a way of answering back that I don't like at all. Speak to her about it, will you, Edith?"

"Oh yes, of course I will."

"I'm afraid my mother spoils them. However, Archie will be going to school soon. Of course it isn't for me to interfere. I have always made a point of letting you do exactly as you like about the children, haven't I, Edith? But I'm beginning to think, really, Dilly ought to have another gov——" He stopped, looking self-conscious.

"Oh, she's only five, quite a baby," said Edith. "I daresay I can manage her for the present. Leave it to me."

Since his return, Edith had never once referred to Bruce's sea-voyage. Once or twice he had thanked her with real gratitude, and even remorse, for the line she had taken, but her one revenge had been to change the subject immediately. If Bruce wished to discuss the elopement that she had so laboriously concealed, he would have to go elsewhere.

A brilliantly coloured version, glittering with success and lurid with melodrama, had been given (greatly against the hearer's will) to Goldthorpe at the club. One of the most annoying things to Bruce was that he was perfectly convinced, when he was confessing the exact truth, that Goldthorpe didn't believe a word of it.

It was unfortunate, too, for Bruce, that he felt it incumbent on him to keep it from Vincy;

and not to speak of the affair at all was a real sacrifice on Vincy's part, also. For they would both have enjoyed discussing it, while Goldthorpe, the only human being in whom Bruce ever really confided, was not only bored but incredulous. He considered Bruce not only tedious to the verge of imbecility, but unreliable beyond the pardonable point of inaccuracy. In fact, Bruce was his ideal of the most wearisome of liars and the most untruthful of bores; and here was poor Vincy dying to hear all about his old friend, Mavis (he never knew even whether she had mentioned his name), ready to revel, with his peculiar humour, in every detail of the strange romance, particularly to enjoy her sudden desertion of Bruce for an unmarried commercial traveller who had fallen in love with her on board.—And yet, it had to be withheld! Bruce felt it would be disloyal, and he had the decency to be ashamed to speak of his escapade to an intimate friend of his wife.

Bruce complained very much of the dullness of the early autumn in London without Aylmer. This sudden mania for long journeys on Aylmer's part was a most annoying hobby. He would never get such a pleasant friend as Aylmer again. Aylmer was his hero.

"Why do you think he's gone away?" he rather irritatingly persisted.

"I haven't the slightest idea."

"Do you know, Edith, it has sometimes occurred to me that if—that, well—well, you know what I mean—if things had turned out differently, and you had done as I asked you——"

"Well?"

"Why, I have a sort of idea," he looked away, "that Aylmer might—well, might have proposed to *you*!"

"Oh! *What* an extraordinary idea!"

"But he never did show any sign whatever, I suppose of—well, of—being more interested in you than he ought to have been?"

"Good heavens, no!"

"Oh, of course, I know that—you're not his style. You liked him very much, didn't you, Edith? . . ."

"I like him very much now."

"However, I doubt if you ever quite appreciated him. He's so full of ability; such an intellectual chap! Aylmer is more a man's man. *I* miss him, of course. He was a very great friend of mine. And he didn't ever at all, in the least—seem to——"

"Seem to what?"

"It would have been a very unfair advantage

to take of my absence if he had," continued Bruce.

"Oh!"

"But he was incapable of it, of course."

"Of course."

"He *never* showed any special interest, then, beyond——"

"Never."

"I was right, I suppose, as usual. You never appreciated him; he was not the sort of man a woman *would* appreciate. . . . But he's a great loss to me, Edith. I need a man who can understand—intellectual sympathy——"

"Mr. Vincy!" announced the servant.

Vincy had not lost his extraordinary gift for turning up at the right moment. He was more welcome than ever now.

THE END

Lightning Source UK Ltd.
Milton Keynes UK
UKHW041920041222
413331UK00002B/113